TWO NAOMIS

Olugbemisola Rhuday-Perkovich & Audrey Vernick

SCHOLASTIC INC.

For all of my sisters, in spirit and in truth
—ORP

For my ever-growing, ever-evolving family
—AV

ISBN 978-1-338-25029-9

12 11 10 9 8 7 6 5 4 3   18 19 20 21 22

Printed in the U.S.A.   40

First Scholastic printing, October 2017

Typography by Torborg Davern

CHAPTER ONE

Naomi Marie

"Third time's the charm, right?" says Ms. Starr. She glances at the clock before she smiles at me. *Sparkles* at me, really, because she's like that.

The library is pretty busy for a sunny Saturday afternoon. The feeling that my little sister, Brianna, calls "the hopies" starts bubbling up inside me. I cross my legs for luck (but at the ankle, so I don't look like I have to pee).

"Do you have to use the restroom?" Ms. Starr asks.

I uncross my legs. "Um . . . just practicing ballet."

"Wow, Naomi! I knew you did West African dance, but ballet too?" She sparkles some more. "On top of everything else? You are such an accomplished young lady!"

I try to look accomplished while I make a mental note to ask Momma if I can take ballet. Then it won't be a lie, just . . . practicing in advance.

I change the subject. "I think the new neon-yellow flyers worked." There has been a huge stack at the circulation desk all week, and now they're gone. I grin and check out the Teen Gamez Crew over at the computers. Brandon Davis is there, even though he's only ten, like me; he throws a smirk in my direction. *Just wait*, I think. *You'll be begging to join my club in about five minutes.*

Don't get me wrong, I like video games and stuff, especially at Uncle Andrew's, because my cousins have all the latest ones PLUS they have a basement playroom, which means it's too much effort for Momma to check on me and make sure I'm not melting my brain. I tell her that my cousins don't seem like their brains have melted (except for Wayne), but she's still all, I Said No. So anyway, I like them, but digital games are nowhere near as good as laughing and talking and eating cookies during Apples to Apples or UNO or Mad Gab. Or doing a Tower of London puzzle. I do all that stuff when I'm with my dad, but now Ms. Starr and I are starting a Bored? Board Games! Club at the library, and even though no one showed up for the first two meetings, the flyers are gone—so it looks like this time they will!

"Third time's definitely the charm!" I say. "I'm going to set up." Maybe we'll even do this twice or three times a week. Then I can hang out here and play games when Momma's friend *who's-a-man-that-she-goes-on-A-LOT-of-dates-(yuck)-with* Tom comes over and Dad's working. This morning, Momma announced that Tom will *bring his daughter* over for lunch one day soon, which probably means I won't be able to hide in my room anymore, so I need this club to happen fast in case that becomes a regular thing.

But that means people have to show up. The clock is working for once, so at 2:51 I go back out to Ms. Starr, who's showing a line of people how to use the self-checkout machine.

"Did we forget to put the time on the flyer?" I ask. "I thought we said two thirty, but it's two fifty-one. . . ."

"Yep, two thirty," says Ms. Starr, trying to scan a chewed-up copy of *Charlie Parker Played Be Bop* before this baby totally loses it. "What time is—" She looks up at the clock. "Oh." She isn't sparkly anymore, but that could be because *Charlie Parker Played Be Bop* is kind of damp. After she hands it to the baby, she wipes her hands on her jeans.

She looks at me. "I'll tell you what, Naomi. As soon as this line goes down, I'll play a round of UNO with you. I bet Ms. Howser will join us too."

I don't want Ms. Howser to join us. She smells like corn chips and got mad at me once for eating a mint in the library. A mint! Anyway, what does she mean, a round of UNO?

"Everyone's just a little late," I say.

She doesn't say anything.

"That whole big stack of flyers is gone!" I say. "Maybe there's a parade or street fair or something that's making people late. There's always a street fair." That's what we figured when no one showed up for the Books about Marine Mammals Club, and the Let's Read in Alphabetical Order Club. Ms. Starr glances over to the Toddler Nook, which has beanbag chairs and allows goldfish eating (the crackers, not the real ones) and sippy cups. I follow her eyes—a bunch of little girls are coloring on sheets of yellow paper. *Neon* yellow, just like . . .

"By this morning, when no one had taken a flyer, I gave some to the kids for coloring. I, uh, thought I'd put them to good use . . . reduce, reuse . . ." Ms. Starr trails off.

Oh.

"I guess everyone who was planning to come . . . ," she says softly, ". . . is already here." She finishes the last scan, and this time I can't look directly at her because my eyes feel a little funny.

"Hey! I've got an idea!" Ms. Starr sparkles again, which must be something they teach in librarian school, because Momma is like that too, especially these days whenever she talks about Tom. She's almost as excited about Tom as she is about Poem in Your Pocket Day. "Let's round up the Teen Gamez Crew for a good game of Life!"

"Thanks, but it's okay, Ms. Starr," I say quickly, trying to sound as cheery as she does. "I have to go. Thanks anyway."

I leave before she can feel even sorrier for me. Now, in addition to ballet, I'm going to have to get my best friend, Xiomara, to come back here with me so Ms. Starr won't think I have no friends. Which means I'll have to watch *Vocalympians!* in return, on account of that's Xiomara's favorite show and she claims to be allergic to books, so she never wants to go to the library. Momma, always the school librarian, gives her books for her birthday, so I use my allowance to buy Xiomara secret presents that she actually wants.

★ ★ ★

I walk to Dad's apartment without even realizing I mean to go there. It's been two years, and it doesn't feel weird anymore having Dad live somewhere else, especially since somewhere else is only five blocks away. Sometimes we even run into him at the grocery store, and even though he and Momma don't hug or anything, they are polite and not screaming and throwing eggs like I heard Meg Kelly's parents do.

Mrs. Hill-Davis steps out to sweep her stoop, but I know she's really keeping an eye on me. I don't mind, so I wave. Dad must have sensed I was coming, because he's just picked up a chicken roti from Ali's—good thing I got here while it's still warm. It's pretty big too, but rotis are kind of hard to share, so it's also a good thing that I am very, very hungry. I stand at the counter and eat it while he makes himself a peanut butter sandwich—well, really a half sandwich, because he only has one slice of bread left. He should plan better.

"Good day?" he asks.

"Sure, I was . . . hanging out at the library," I say. I leave it at that.

After we eat, we start the puzzle on the coffee table without saying a word. Momma would have asked me seventeen hundred questions by now: Who was there? Did I have fun? Did I pick up a book list and remember to say thank you? Dad is just ready with a seventeen-hundred-piece puzzle of the Brooklyn Bridge. I want to say thank you, but me and my dad tend to say a lot without really saying it; I smile as I pick up an H-shaped piece.

"So how's everything?" Dad asks after I send Momma a text to let her know where I am. She sends back smiley faces with a kiss, which I really need.

I never know how to answer questions like that. What am I supposed to say if one thing was bad? Or two things were good, but seven were horrible? So I say, "Fine." But then I remember. "Um, well. There's one thing. . . ." I'm not sure how to say this. I mean, both Momma and Dad have been going on dates and whatever (gross), but now it seems like I should say something about Tom since he's going to be sitting at our table and eating off the plates that Grandma Billie bought. "Well . . . Tom's coming over for lunch or something. Maybe just a snack. And we're going to meet his daughter." I shrug as I say it, to show him how not-happy-but-not-going-to-be-rude I am, so he knows whose side I'm on.

"Oh yes! Your mom mentioned that. I'm . . . glad it's working out." Yeah, right. He looks as glad as Xiomara's dog, Shotsie, did when she had to wear that plastic cone around her neck for three weeks. I shrug again and finish a corner of the puzzle.

"I *am* glad, really, Naomi," he says after a pause. "Of course, I won't say I'm glad that it didn't work for your mom and me to be married, but I'm glad we can always be a family. In a different way now. I want to know that *you're* okay with everything."

Ugh, parents and "everything." But I've had lots of practice with this, because Momma asks me almost every day if I'm okay with "everything." "I'm fine," I say.

He goes on. "And I'm especially glad that we can have these hangouts any time you want."

I hug him. Mostly, the "transition" has been pretty easy on me and Brianna; she was only two years old when Dad moved out, and everybody knows about the Terrible Twos—she didn't care much about anything back then except touching my stuff and showing the entire world her "big girl" panties. Now she's four and not much has changed, except the panties thing. Thankfully. Robbie Jenkins still eats booger cookies, and he's seven.

But still, the whole Tom thing is weird. Like I'm not sure how nice to be, on account of my dad. But I also don't want Momma thinking I'm being rude to her . . . friend. From far away, Tom's okay, I guess. I don't hate him. He likes to tell jokes, and he doesn't mind when you don't laugh, because he knows they're not that funny. But Momma looked so nervous and also excited when she was talking about him and his daughter coming for lunch that I could tell she's starting to *really* want me to laugh at those jokes. And she kept saying how she thought his daughter and I would get along because his daughter is a checkers champ and I'm a chess champ, and I guess it isn't supposed to matter that they are two completely different games.

It's probably a good thing that no one showed up at the library today. I'm going to have my hands full taking care of my parents. And that won't exactly be fun and games.

CHAPTER TWO

Naomi E.

"Why did your mom leave the no-head ladies here?" My best friend, Annie, and I are packing up what was once Mom's sewing room. And what Dad promises will soon be our library/TV/music/relax-and-also-we'll-be-allowed-to-eat-in-there room.

"You can't take no-head ladies on a plane," I explain. "There are rules about what you can take on planes." Mom, by the way, doesn't call them no-head ladies. To her they are the mannequins. Or dress forms. Also, they aren't only missing heads. They have no arms or legs either. She uses them when she designs costumes, which is her job.

"I know about planes," Annie says. "I went to North Carolina last summer, and they didn't let me bring the milk shake I had just bought through that security thing, which makes no sense, because what problem is a milk shake going to make?"

It's a good question.

Mom went to California three months ago because she was offered a great job making costumes for a movie. She had to get there in a hurry. She brought what she knew she'd need right away: sketch pads, her laptop, her lucky eraser. Months before that, when Mom and Dad got separated and then divorced, she wasn't in such a hurry. And she still hasn't moved all her sewing stuff out of our house. So now we're packing it up to send to her, because it looks like she's going to be in California for a while.

Annie and I have been working for almost an hour, and the room doesn't look any more like a library/TV/music/relax-and-also-we'll-be-allowed-to-eat-in-there room than it did before we started. Well, one box is filled up with ribbons and material and thread and stuff—that one's ready to be taped and labeled.

"Gnomes, we should take a break." Without waiting to see if I agree, Annie pats a no-head lady on the shoulder and heads toward my room.

No one but Annie calls me Gnomes. To be honest, I always thought she was calling me Nomes, a pretty good nickname for Naomi, which is a really hard name to nick. But one time she handed me a note, and she'd written "Gnomes" because she thinks those ugly little elf things some of our neighbors have on their small front lawns are actually cute. Whenever she says it, I hear it as Nomes. Because Nomes is better.

"Wanna 'read'?"

"Reading" is different from regular reading. It started when Annie's grandparents sent her family a huge box of books. Annie and her brothers were excited—there were so many books! But they were all in German—which no one in her family speaks. Annie never figured that one out. But it was the beginning of our "reading" tradition: Annie takes a book with lots of pictures and tells the story of the pictures. She does it with our English-language books too. It's why I kept so many of my old picture books.

She moves my old stuffed animal Lambikins and slides a book out of my bookcase. "This," she says, "is the story of a mouse in a dress and red shoes beneath a banana tree." I know that's *NOT* what the story is, but she's right—that's what the cover shows.

I smile.

"A baby mouse sleeps in a crib beneath a duck. And sleeps some more. Then lots of things happen that aren't interesting."

She starts laughing, because this is one of our favorite books from when we were little, and everything in it was incredibly interesting to us then. And the thing about Annie is that she never laughs a little. I know I'll be waiting awhile for her to continue, and even though I try to keep a straight face, her laughing makes me laugh too.

She tries to get it together. "The girl mouse writes a word over and over and then dances with three butterflies."

That sets me off, because the butterflies are just in the art and have nothing to do with the story. But then she drops the book, says, "I'm hungry," and is off.

Annie has the refrigerator door pulled open and is staring inside, like she lives here. I love that. She *should* live here. She'd be my perfect sister. And she'd definitely rather have me for a sibling than Leo and Chase because, *ugh*. Her brothers are gross.

Dad looks miserable, with envelopes and letters spread all over the table. Then he piles the papers up and shoves them into a big folder. "Hungry?" he asks. Because of the refrigerator hint. And because we're in the kitchen. And because Annie is always hungry.

"Wait. Naomi, did we have lunch? Were we supposed to give Annie lunch?" We don't go hungry, my dad and me, but I'm pretty sure there are some days when we have five meals and some when maybe we have two or even one and also a lot of snacks. Dad and I are champions of snacking.

"I'm fine," Annie says, straight into the refrigerator. "Ate before I came over."

"I had an apple," I say. I don't mention that I cut it and arranged the pieces around a big puddle of chocolate syrup, because Dad thinks apples and chocolate don't go together, which is all kinds of crazy.

"You know what you should do?" Dad asks. He doesn't care that we don't answer. "You should go outside."

Annie is still standing in front of the open refrigerator, looking in, not moving.

"It finally dried out from all the rain. You can take a break from packing up Mom's stuff. Or are you done? Is it ready to go?"

I shake my head no and gently close the refrigerator, pulling Annie out of the spell she seems to have fallen under. I grab a bag of popcorn from the pantry and say, "Come on."

My backyard is tiny, but I love, love, love it. Our house is attached to another on one side—it's called a row house—but it's also on a corner, so it gets a lot of sun. It has an old swing set that Annie and I have played on forever, and everything about it fits us exactly right.

In the back corner, where the sun shines for most of the day in the summer, I have my own garden. Last summer I grew strawberries and tomatoes. I loved picking them when every last bit of green faded away and they were the perfect shade of ready-to-eat red. When they're ripe, you almost don't have to pull—they practically drop into your hand. It makes me so happy to watch tiny little plants with a few leaves grow into . . . food! And I love the way the big leaves on a tomato plant smell like tomato even before there's the tiniest little tomato growing there.

Annie grabs a soccer ball (it's hers, but she keeps it at my house) and kicks it in circles around the tree. Yes, our tiny perfect backyard has a tree. Only one. But in the spring, in just a few weeks, it will bloom with pink blossoms, and two years ago there were actual apricots that were beautiful. They tasted awful, but they were great to look at.

"Next weekend, on Saturday, do you want to come over?" Annie has what I call soccer feet. She usually can't keep them still. But now she stops the ball and lies on her stomach on the swing next to mine. Like a little flying superhero, she pushes up. "It's Chase's birthday party so we're skipping soccer, and Mom said you could come."

I'm smiling and nodding yes, because it's what I WANT to do, but I'm also remembering that Dad said next Saturday I have to meet a lady, not the no-head kind. Someone he has been seeing a lot. She has two kids, daughters. And for some reason, it's really important that we have a meal together.

"I wish," I say. "I have to go with my dad to have lunch with Valentine, I think her name is. His new lady friend."

"Lady *with* a head probably, right?"

"Probably." I smile. Annie's the best. The best best friend.

And without even saying a word, because that's how it is with best friends, Annie kicks the soccer ball to its spot by the back door, and we both go back inside, to Mom's sewing room. Because I want to be there, and Annie somehow gets that. I really want to be with my mom, but being with her stuff is better than not being with her at all.

CHAPTER THREE

Naomi Marie

"Why aren't you wearing a fancy dress?" asks Brianna for the seven hundredth time. "Momma said this was a special 'cay-zhun. That means 'fancy.'"

"I haven't decided what to wear, and it's occasion, and it's not, actually. It's only lunch. With Tom." I turn away and mutter, "Big whoop," so she can't hear.

"I'm telling," sings Brianna, who has magic supersonic ears whenever I don't want her to.

"Of course you are," I answer. Momma is wearing the long skirt she got at the Dance Africa festival last year. Like it's a holiday or something! "Come on, you have to clean up all these Legos and clay," I say.

"I can't. I'll mess up my fancy dress. If you put yours on, then neither one of us will have to clean up!" Brianna happy-dances, and I join her for a few seconds because that's pretty good thinking for four years old. I've taught her well.

Still. "It doesn't work that way," I say, holding out the Legos bin. Being four must be nice. I don't remember. Because ten is all about being responsible. Like cleaning up your room to play nicely with Tom's daughter, though she may not even be capable of playing nicely. But no one is thinking of that, are they? No, they aren't.

Momma has been so nervous and jumpy and making fancy Thanksgiving food, even though it's nowhere near Thanks-giving, just because Tom and his probably mean daughter are coming over today. I even had to miss my Saturday-morning library visit! Which is always a great follow-up to my Friday-afternoon visit, because lots can happen in between. But nooooo, even though Tom's daughter probably hates libraries, I have to be neat and polite. And I will. Because I am responsible. I will hold my head high like Queen Nefertiti and smile (only a small one) and remember to put my napkin in my lap, but I will not, I repeat, NOT wear a fancy dress. Take that, mean library-hating daughter of Tom-who-needs-to-make-his-own-lunch.

She is not even dressed up! Tom's daughter has on a purple shirt with a bear holding a sign that says California, and old jeans, and she's carrying a gray sweatshirt. What she doesn't have is a smile, and I'm standing there with mine on, all big and fake just like

Mrs. Banco on the first day of second grade, right before she yelled at Sarafina Wilson for crying.

In addition to my smile, I have on my skating jacket and leggings with the cool red swirls. I'm actually a little hot, but I think my skating outfit makes me look strong and confident, like a girl in a poster. Plus it has a tiny hole that no one but me knows about. So there. I do have on the dangly gold earrings Nana gave me, which I usually save for special occasions, but also for days when I need to be brave. I almost wore my "Daddy's Girl" T-shirt. But that would be mean, and I don't want to be mean, like Tom's daughter probably is.

"Hi, guys, come on in," says Momma in a really loud voice.

Which is maybe why, when Tom's daughter says hi, it seems really quiet. I *hope* that's why and not because she has, like, quietude, which is a good way of pretending you're behaving when you're actually thinking uncooperative thoughts. I can beat anyone at the quietude game. I narrow my eyes.

"Hi, girls!" booms Tom, like a ringmaster.

"Hi!" Brianna yells back. So I say hi too, in my quiet-but-not-quietude voice, because Momma is giving me a look.

They start taking off their shoes, and I look down. "Hey!" I blurt out. "I have those in red!" Tom's daughter has green high-tops with purple laces, the same ones I got last week. I point to mine on the shoe rack by the door.

"Cool! I got mine last week," she says, and there isn't any attitude, so maybe she's only feeling the same way I am, which is WEIRD.

"You have good taste," I say, and I smile a real smile, to make things a little less WEIRD.

We all move into the living room and stand looking at each other until Brianna flops down on the couch; then everyone else fake-laughs and sits down.

"Well, isn't that funny," says Momma, glancing at Tom. She laughs a tinkly, fairy godmother laugh just like Mrs. Driscoll before she gave us that pop quiz on all the bridges in New York City. Tom laughs too, and clears his throat.

"What?" me and Tom's daughter say. At the same time. Heh.

"Well," says Tom, "it's quite funny, because we already have quite a coincidence here. . . ." He trails off.

"Dad, it's not like they only made one pair," his daughter says, and we catch each other's eyes because, PARENTS. Once Momma met some lady at the bodega who was buying the same brand of toilet paper and had a son who used to go to my school, and they were all, What an Amazing Coincidence. And when I said that actually it didn't seem that remarkable to me, all I got was a side-eye from Momma and no points for using the word *remarkable* in a sentence.

"Oh, it's not the shoes," says Momma. "It's, well . . . we thought this would be *such* a *funny* little surprise for you girls. We've been waiting to tell you. . . ." She trails off too, and I can tell Tom's daughter is getting as scared as I am, because we both say "WHAT!!!!????" in very loud voices.

Momma and Tom look at each other again, and oh my goodness, if I were stalling like this, Momma would be calling me *Naomi Marie*, which she usually does when she's either really mad or really glad about something I did.

"Naomi, meet . . . ," Momma starts in a low voice, like when she's about to tell me that we're actually not going out for pizza but having leftovers instead.

"Naomi!!!!" Tom finishes, like he's actually taking us out for pizza. Which he isn't.

Whoa. He must be really nervous. Naomi? He can't even remember his own daughter's name. A teeny tiny bit of *Poor Tom* pops up in me.

"What's *her* name?" Brianna says, pointing to Tom's daughter.

"That's it!" says Momma, laughing harder and faker. She grabs Tom's hand, which makes me not feel that *Poor Tom* for him anymore. "Naomi, meet Naomi!"

"We have two Naomis!" Tom says, smiling like he just got birthday cake on a regular day.

Wait, *what?!!!*

Brianna starts to cry.

CHAPTER FOUR

Naomi E.

It wasn't cool of Dad to keep that secret. A secret with Valerie. Secret from me.

But it's not like I'm going to cry about it.

When the crier finally catches her breath, she says, "How come Naomi gets a twin and I don't?" Which makes no sense at all.

"We're not twins," I say in maybe not my nicest voice. "We just have the same name!" I walk over to the couch where she's sprawled. "What's your name?"

She sits up and wipes her nose with the back of her hand. Ew. "Brianna."

"Didn't you ever meet another Brianna?" The other Naomi

walks over to us, like maybe I should back off her sister or something even though I'm only trying to help.

"Remember in your dance class?" she asks. "Brianna T. and Brianna W.?"

Brianna sits up straight on the couch, and her feet stick straight out. It makes her look so little. I use a nicer voice.

"See?" I say. "And you weren't twins, right?"

"I'll say," the other Naomi says. "Those two had to get lots of Reminders, remember?" Then they look at each other in this we're-sisters-and-you-wouldn't-understand kind of way.

"Naomi," Dad says way too loudly. "I mean, my Naomi. Why don't you show Naomi and Brianna what we brought?"

Cookies!! Before this day took a turn for the weird, Dad and I went to Morningstar. It's the best bakery in the world. Every time Dad and I walk in, Stefan or Sheera or Bessie starts making his coffee and asks me "Croissant or bagel today, Naomi?" And today, after breakfast, I got to pick out a pound of their amazing butter cookies, with chocolate sprinkles, rainbow sprinkles, colored sugars, chocolate chips, and royal icing.

I take the box—tied with that cool bakery string—to Brianna, because Dad is practically pointing at her with his head.

The box doesn't look as nice as it did when we left Morningstar. There are some greasy stains, which just shows how buttery and perfect those cookies are if you take a second to think about it.

"Is this cupcakes?" she asks, sort of grabbing the box away from me.

"No, really great cookies," I say, looking to the other Naomi, hoping she can help.

"I love cookies," she says. "Almost every kind."

"Me too!" Maybe this Naomi and I can escape the little sister. This is all weird enough without having to worry about hurting someone's feelings just by having a name.

"Except," she says, and then at the same time we say, "peanut butter."

Dad and Valerie laugh way too loud.

"But wait a minute," the other Naomi says, her eyes on the box of cookies. Then she looks at her mom and stops.

Valerie gently shakes her head.

"But what?" I ask.

"Nothing . . . did you ever meet another Naomi before?" she asks me.

"One time," I say. "At my cousin's Bat Mitzvah. She was a great dancer."

That makes Brianna jump up and start dancing. Naomi looks ready to join her, but she glances at me and then at her mom and asks, "Can we eat now?"

Then it's all sorts of time-for-lunch action as Valerie asks her daughters to help, leaving me with Dad, standing near the table, already set for five, not knowing what to do. Would it feel less weird if they were at our house for lunch? Because here they know everything and I don't even know where to sit. Or where the bathroom is. But then, if we did have them over for lunch, there'd be a good chance Dad would completely forget to give them any food. And then that baby might cry even more.

Valerie, Brianna, and the other Naomi bring out an amazing feast—enough food for fifteen people, I bet. Really cheesy mac and cheese, big soft rolls, colorful salads, rice and peas, chicken! I wonder if maybe they only have meals once a day like Dad and I sometimes do, though with us it's usually by accident.

I serve myself plenty of everything because it all looks so delicious. And beautiful too on my big yellow plate.

We're all busy eating when Dad reaches for a second roll and asks, "How's that new program at the library going, Naomi?"

I try to remember what program at the library. And it's quiet while everyone waits for me to answer.

Finally, Valerie says, "Naomi Marie? He's talking to you."

The Naomi that's her daughter asks, "How'd he know about that?" She looks down at her food.

How is anyone supposed to know who they're talking about, or to? But also, why does Dad know about some program Valerie's kid is doing at a library? He can't even remember which days I have gym.

The Naomi he was talking to, the one who isn't me, shrugs. We eat in quiet for a little while. Then Valerie says, "I hear you like playing checkers, Naomi," which I think she said to me.

What is she even talking about? Did Dad tell her how I beat his friend Loofie three times in a row? Who even cares? I mean, if someone is going to know one thing about me, it shouldn't have anything to do with checkers.

It could be that my mom is working on a cool movie, and I can't wait to visit her and maybe even go on the set. Or that I read *Charlotte's Web* four times last summer. Or that Annie and I once wrote a play called *You're Too Tall and We Don't Understand!* and we sold tickets and performed it in her backyard.

Checkers is something like 832nd on the list of important things about me.

"Yeah," I say. And then I get really serious about eating. Because I can't be expected to talk when I'm eating.

"Can I be escused?" Brianna asks, and I want to say, "It's *excused*," and would you believe that's exactly what the other Naomi says?

"Well, I suppose you could," Valerie says. "But then you'd miss those delicious cookies Tom and Naomi brought. So why don't you help clear the dishes?"

I stand to clear my plate when Brianna says, "Why did you say cookies? What about the coconut cake?"

"We'll be having the wonderful cookies that Tom and Naomi were thoughtful enough to bring." Valerie's teeth are clenched even when she's talking, and I am certain her eyes, staring straight at Brianna, could not possibly be open any wider.

"Could we have both?" the other Naomi asks. "Cookies and coconut cake?"

I don't like coconut cake, so I don't really see what the big deal is.

Dad says, "Valerie, if you made something special, then by all means, please serve it. Save the cookies for another day."

"But I—"

Dad doesn't let me finish. "I've always wanted to try your coconut cake."

I whisper, probably a little too loudly, "I don't like coconut cake." The truth is, I've never even tasted it. But I don't usually like coconut anything. And I want those cookies. And if she isn't going to serve them, I want her to close that box right up and wrap the string around it again and hand it back to me so we can take it home.

Everyone heard me. It's quiet for a little too long. Finally, Valerie says, "Let's have both. It's a special occasion, having Naomi and Tom over for the first time."

"I told you it was a special 'cay-zhun," Brianna says to her sister. "You should of wored a dress. Not the skating clothes with the hole."

"Hey, um," the other Naomi says to me in a really sweet voice, "you should taste my mom's cake, just a tiny taste. Everyone loves it."

So I kind of have to. And I guess it is pretty good. But I can't make myself eat more than that one bite. That doesn't keep me from eating cookies. Seven of them.

When we leave, Valerie puts all the extra cookies and one big piece of coconut cake into the Morningstar box to take home. Knowing Dad, that will be our lunch tomorrow. Mmm.

CHAPTER FIVE

Naomi Marie

"Are you awake yet?"

"No." I pull my comforter all the way up over my head. I haven't slept a real sleep since last Saturday's lunch "surprise."

"Then how come you talked?"

"Because you woke me up."

"But—"

"If you don't leave me alone, I'll tell Momma about the peanut butter you put in Rahel's hair."

"You told me to!"

"Everybody knows you don't put peanut butter in doll hair. But I'll still tell. So leave me alone."

"You're not supposed to tretten me. I'm telling."

ARGH!!!! I sit up and throw my small yellow pillow at Bri's head. "Hello, I'm trying to sleep, doughnut hole! *And* the word is *threaten*, as in *this*." I make a scary face at her.

She throws the pillow back at me and climbs into the bed next to me. "So do you want to play school instead? I can be the teacher now."

I give up. "Okay, but . . . it's bedschool. That means the students get to lie down the whole time."

"Okay. My name is Mrs. Vitamin C. Welcome to my bedschool. What's your name, little girl?"

"Naomi," I mumble. "And I have a condition where I keep my eyes closed."

"Welcome, Naomi! There's another Naomi in this class too. You can be Black Naomi, and she can be White Naomi. I think you should be line partners!"

I roll out of bed to the floor. "*I'm* Naomi," I say. "And I'm not being line partners with anyone. I'm not even playing anymore." I wait for Bri to cry and call Momma.

She gets out of my bed and sits next to me. "Want to play something else?"

"No."

"Are you sleeping again?"

I pull a pillow down and hold it over my head until I hear her leave. Then I feel bad, because she's going to be gone all day anyway, for a playdate with her friend Nef, while Momma takes Xiomara and me to the natural history museum.

I love days like this. No school on a Wednesday! Woot! It's like a little weekend smack in the middle of the week. The teachers still have to go to school and do meetings or something, which is maybe what made grouchhead Ms. Horvath give us homework, but at least it's project homework. A Penobscot artist from Maine visited our class last week and showed us these beautiful baskets made from brown ash trees. Now Xiomara and I are doing a presentation on Penobscot basketmaking traditions, and we can do a lot of research at the museum, so today we're combining a day-off playdate with team homework. Woot! Woot!

Momma pokes her head in. "Sorry, sweetie pie. I gather from little Miss Vitamin C's report that she woke you up. I was going to give you another half hour."

"That's okay," I say. "I want to get up and get ready anyway. What time is Nef's mom picking up Brianna? We should get to the museum early." I haven't told Momma yet that my list of things to do today includes a Shake Shack lunch after the museum. And the Maker Magic Playground. Also maybe ice cream. I checked the weather twice last night, and it's supposed to go up to 75 degrees. That sounds like ice cream weather to me, especially if Xiomara and I do a good job of being *industrious*. Maybe I can drop that word into our conversation for bonus points.

"Nef might be coming down with something," says Momma. "We can't send Bri over there. I'm sorry."

Noooo! "So she's coming with us? What about Dad?"

"He's got conference calls all day," says Momma. "But he wants you to know that he would definitely rather hang out under the blue whale with you." The whale room is my favorite part of the museum. It's so calm, and the whale songs are playing so softly you don't even realize it, but you *feel* it.

"So . . . it's time to be flexible and creative again, right?" I mumble, folding my arms. Then I unfold them and hold them straight out in the most unflexible way I can.

Momma comes and sits on the bed next to me. "And . . . Xiomara's not coming."

"WHAT?! Why not?" I flop down onto my back.

"Her parents need her at the store," Momma says. "She and Kwame are going to help with inventory."

"Aren't there child labor laws against that or something?" I grumble. This day is really losing its woot. "And we were going to the museum to do research for our project," I say. "Now we'll get a bad grade, and we won't go to college. Everything's ruined."

"We're still going to the museum," Momma says, laughing.

I sigh. "Momma, Bri's going to get lost and need to go to the bathroom every five seconds. And then you'll be so busy watching her you won't be able to help me."

"Not to worry!" says Momma, with a big smile on her face. "I've called in reinforcements."

I'm ten and Growing Up, so . . . "I get it. . . . Are we having Ladies' Family Day again? Ooh! Does that mean Auntie Evelyn is coming?"

". . . Not exactly."

"What do you mean?"

"Well, I just talked to Tom, and—"

"Momma!"

"... we thought that it would be nice if we made this—"

"NO WAY." I fold my arms again. Momma sighs, and I put the pillow back over my head. I hear Bri return.

"Is her condition over?" she whispers. She runs to the bed and climbs on top of me. "NAOMI NAOMI WE'RE GOING TO THE MUSEUM TOGETHER WITH TOM AND WHITE NAOMI! WE CAN PLAY MUSEUM SCHOOL!"

"I think I'm going to be sick," I mumble. Momma snuggle-kisses me, but I refuse to smile.

Woot Wednesday is now officially the Worst Wednesday for real.

We're museum members, but there's still a long wait. While we stand on line, I take out my notebook and read over the list I made yesterday. I did flower doodles all over it and drew a smiling sun wearing tap shoes at the bottom. It reads:

1. Sleep Late
2. Brianna Leaves
3. Xiomara Comes Over!
4. Museum Trip with Xiomara and Momma!
5. Shake Shack!
6. Playground!
7. Ice Cream!

I crumple it up and toss it in a nearby trash can. I'm making a new list in my head now:

1. Everybody in the world decided to spend their Woot Wednesday at the Museum of Natural History.
2. Brianna whines and keeps dropping Rahel on purpose.
3. Momma says we can see the 3D movie, but it's sold out all day because EVERYBODY is at the museum.
4. We meet Tom and the Other Naomi inside, and Tom hugs Momma so tight I'm sure she needs CPR.
5. The Other Naomi and I don't hug. And when Momma says *"Oh, it would have been cute if you were both wearing your matching shoes!"* the Other Naomi looks like she made the same promise that I did NEVER to wear them again.
6. Brianna gets lost in the rocks and minerals room.
7. By the time we find Brianna, she has to go to the bathroom.
8. Momma keeps whispering at me to walk with the Other Naomi, but the Other Naomi is being slow and draggy and full of quietude.
9. Brianna gets lost in the Hall of Ocean Life.
10. Momma and Tom are so busy making googly eyes at each other that they keep letting Brianna get lost.
11. Brianna drops Rahel in the Hall of New York State Environment, so we have to spend forever wandering around the most boring part of the museum.
12. The Other Naomi keeps talking about how the Met is more fun, so even though I love the Met, I have to pretend I don't.

"My dad's been promising to take me to the Costume Institute for weeks!" she says. "Instead we came here."

"You can probably still go there today if you walk a little faster," I say.

"But then your sister will get lost," she answers right back with a smirk.

Well.

I march ahead, until finally, I get to the special pre-European contact exhibit. . . and there's no basket section. Well, there's something, all right. A sign that says: Currently closed for repairs.

ARGH!!!!!!!

Momma and Tom run up.

"Did your sister come this way?" Momma asks.

The Other Naomi strolls over. "Again?"

Momma tells us to Stay Where We Are, which is the rule of always, and she and Tom go off to track down Bri.

The Other Naomi does a whole lot of eye rolling and sighing.

Momma and Tom return, with Bri dragging behind them.

I grab Bri's hand, even though I'm mad at her. "When I was little," I whisper, "I used to wish I could spend the night here, just like this book I read."

"That was *the Met*," says the Girl Who Was Not Even in the Conversation.

"I know that," I say. "I meant sleeping over in a museum, any museum." Before she says anything else, I add, "Did you know there are scavenger hunts at the Met?"

I can tell she didn't; she looks away. Now it's my turn to smirk, but I don't because I'm mature. I just do it in my head.

We make it to the exit with everything—my sister, Rahel, and all the Other Naomi's Bad Attitude.

But something's missing.

We could have turned this day into an adventure, Momma, me, and Bri. The two-and-a-half Musketeers.

We would have been Us.

"Is that thunder?" Momma asks Tom, who is not one of Us.

Bri starts to cry.

"This is great," mutters the Other Naomi. "Best day off ever—NOT."

I step forward and stand all the way outside so that no one can see I'm crying too.

CHAPTER SIX

Naomi E.

This museum is the reason so many kids hate museums. It is so boring. But today it's also crowded and *hot*. Valerie's family doesn't have coats or sweaters, so they seem comfortable and happy, while I sweat and lug around the sweatshirt Dad always makes me bring, like we might be attacked by a sudden cold front.

"Have you seen Rahel?" Valerie asks me.

"Who's Rahel?" I say.

"Brianna's doll. Wait here. Your dad and I are going to retrace our steps."

So I stay where I am, looking at birds of New York, thinking of what I'd rather be doing, like hanging out with Annie.

Homework. Maybe a dentist appointment. Or a blood test.

"Are you into birds or something?" the other Naomi asks in an unfriendly voice.

"No. Your mother said to wait here while they go find your sister's missing doll. At least it's not your sister missing. Again."

"She's little," the other Naomi says. "You probably lost stuff when you were little."

I keep my eyes locked on a big ugly pigeon and its disgusting raw-looking feet. "When I was too little for museums, my parents didn't bring me to them."

She just stares at me like I called her whole family stupid. Maybe I did.

"Okay, Naomi, Naomi," Valerie calls, motioning with her arm for us to follow. Brianna holds up a doll and waves it around.

We all have to go to the whole other side of the museum to see a certain boring thing because the other Naomi has to do homework about it, and when we finally get there, to the whole reason she dragged Dad and me here, it's closed.

Dad and Valerie, who were ahead of us, start walking back the other way, their eyes searching for a missing four-year-old.

"Again?" I say.

I'm about ready to burst into tears by the time they get back with the wandering Brianna.

And even though I'd bet the other Naomi is as annoyed as I am, she acts all *we're sisters and you're not* on me again, taking Brianna's hand and loud-whispering, because she totally wants me to hear. "When I was little," she says, "I used to wish I could spend the night here, just like this book I read."

"That was *the Met*," I remind her, because everyone knows that. And then they keep on talking in that sister way, to remind me that they're this pair and I have nothing to do with it. As if I'd ever want to.

All I want is to leave this hot and crowded museum. And finally, we do. But not until after we go to some secret coat room, where Valerie and her whole family left their bags and sweatshirts and everything. It would have been nice of them to tell me I could leave my sweatshirt there on this boiling-hot day.

"Is that thunder?" Valerie asks Dad as she hands him a big bakery box.

Brianna starts to cry. Of course.

"I don't think so," Dad says, even though I'm pretty sure it was. "Let's give it a try. Let's go to the park."

The sky is not looking friendly, but Dad and Valerie are ignoring it. "Why don't we find a place to sit, and then we can have some snacks. Maybe play some games," Valerie says.

"The ice cream man is sometimes on the corner," Brianna tells me, like she's older than me. Or knows this park better than I do.

"I know. I come here a lot," I say. I follow Valerie and my dad to a bench near a ratty-looking sandbox. Valerie starts unpacking water bottles and Dad opens the big bakery box, and inside there are doughnuts! Well, all right then!

"I brought checkers," Valerie says. "I know you like to play."

"Yeah," the other Naomi says. "Aren't you some kind of checkers champ?"

If I were Valerie, I'd tell the other Naomi to wipe the nasty right out of her voice. But why do they keep saying that? I don't really care about checkers. "I play with my dad's friend Loofie sometimes, I guess, but I'm not a champ."

Valerie looks like I hurt her feelings. Because I don't love checkers?

Dad gives me a look that says something like *Act like you want to be here*. Which is a lot like saying, *Lie, Naomi!*

"That was thoughtful of you," Dad says to Valerie even though he's staring right at me, making me think I was supposed to thank her for bringing some game I don't really want to play.

Valerie passes the doughnuts around, and we each take one. These are not regular doughnuts. They look really great and each one's different and, okay, yeah, my mouth is watering. I pick one with a lot of white glaze on it, and when I bite into it, ugh, it's coconut. It didn't have the flakes! Or the smell! There was no way to know!

I place it on the napkin Valerie gave me and leave it on my lap.

"Did you bring chess too or just checkers?" the other Naomi asks.

"This set has both." Valerie hands a big box to her Naomi. "Why don't you and Naomi—"

"This one's missing the queen," Naomi says, with a mean

look at her sister, who may be burying her doll in the sandbox.

"It wasn't my fault," Brianna says. "I was playing princess family with Rahel and we needed a queen mother and I couldn't find any other queen and Naomi once showed me which one was the chess queen and they don't look alike but it was the only queen I could find!"

I'm about to ask the other Naomi if she wants to play checkers, mostly because I can't listen to that baby cry again and maybe we could set up on another bench and get far away from all this and start over. But then the other Naomi says, "You are not allowed to touch my chess pieces—" And then sure enough Brianna's crying and my father looks at me and I start to feel like it's my fault.

I take the chess and checkers box and open it up while Valerie's hugging Brianna's head and the other Naomi is looking mean and I sit on the grass and start to set up the checkerboard, really to have something to do, because this is super-awkward.

"Who are you playing with?" the other Naomi asks.

I think I feel a raindrop fall as I set the last two red checkers on their black squares. "You?" I ask.

She says, "I don't play checkers. Maybe Brianna will. That's more the kind of game she plays."

Which is a mean thing to say. And I'm about to tell her when the skies open and the rain comes down in a huge rushing gush of water—like it forgot it's supposed to be in drops.

If the weather was trying to send us a message, that message would be "You all should not be trying to spend time together outdoors." Or, I might add, indoors either.

Dad and Valerie make some weird motions at each other, pointing, shrugging, and then waving; and Valerie throws the big box of doughnuts away before she even notices I chose the wrong kind and want another one. And Brianna's crying, and that other Naomi keeps giving me a stink eye like even the rain was all my fault.

CHAPTER SEVEN

Naomi Marie

"Is it my turn now?" asks Brianna. She's already holding a wooden spoon, ready to stir the batter while I supervise. Momma has plugged in the waffle iron, so I'm waiting for the green light to tell me it's ready. I tie on my red apron as usual.

"Okay," I say, helping her onto the stool at the kitchen counter. "But you have to follow my instructions exactly." I pat her head. I've been feeling very big-sisterish all week. After all the not-so-fun surprises lately, and She-Who-Shall-Not-Be-Named being so mean to Brianna, which only I'm allowed to do (even though I'm not really mean to Bri—I mostly need to remind her of who's boss), all I want is to do the things we always do the way we always do them.

Saturday mornings, I make waffles. Bri gets to stir ten times. I wear my red apron and matching red chef's hat. I might also need to remind Momma how great everything is just the way it is, so I'm being a teeny bit extra nice to Bri too.

"Here you go," I say, plopping my chef's hat on her head. "Only for today."

Her eyes get all big like I've turned from Cinderella's stepsister into her fairy godmother. Little sisters like to be all exaggerate-y like that. "You can pour the syrup on your own waffles too," I say. "And maybe mine, IF you do a good job with the stirring."

Of course she gets all excited and starts splattering batter everywhere. "Maybe we can make waffles for Tom and the other Naomi!" she says. "And you guys can be like twins because you are so the same!"

I grab my hat and the spoon, and maybe sort of shove her off the stool. "I changed my mind, cheese head," I say, because I know how much she hates being reminded that her name is also a cheese. Because she hates cheese. Because she's a little sister, and she is weird. "You're just making a big mess!"

"Mooooommaaaa!" she yells. "Naomi's being bossy!"

"No I'm not," I yell too. "I'm showing leadership skills!" Then I whisper, "And I know that *I'm* not a stinky Frenchy cheese."

"Mooommmmmaaaaa!"

Momma doesn't really get that mad. She just finishes making the waffles, and we all sit down. Then Bri sings a dumb song about big sisters that doesn't even make sense, and I cover her mouth with my hand and get in trouble because I am disrespecting her body. So I accidentally on purpose pour all the syrup on MY waffles so there's none left right when Bri asks for it, then Momma says I have to share mine, but Bri doesn't want them because she says they're too soggy and also because she is a little sister. She cries and Momma sighs and it is NOT a regular Saturday morning at all.

After Momma makes us all some cornmeal porridge, which is kind of a punishment breakfast if you ask me, she lets Bri go play while I have to help clean up. I guess I'm Cinderella now.

"We haven't talked much about Tom and Na—his daughter," Momma says for the seven hundredth time. "You've been really busy after school these days."

"Dad and I are working on a big puzzle," I say. "And we have that chess competition coming up, so I do challenges with Ms. A. and the team, and you know, I have to help out at the library. . . ."

I scrape the plates while she starts loading the dishwasher. There's a lot of soggy waffle going into the trash. "I'm sorry about the syrup," I say. "I know it's wrong to waste food."

"Your waffles are some of the highlights of the week," Momma says, kissing my forehead. "And I appreciate the way you've taken on a leadership role with breakfast on Saturdays."

I shrug. "Well, Bri totally messed with me today. I'll make really nice ones next Saturday. It'll be back to normal. Like always. Just us three."

Momma gives me a look. "Little sisters can be a challenge," she says. "And so can big ones." Momma is the middle sister, and according to her, that's the worst. Aunt Bell and Aunt Karen seem okay to me. They always bring bun and cheese or coconut candy when they come over. What they never bring are any same-named people who don't even belong in the apartment.

"Did you and . . . Tom's daughter get a chance to talk a little on our outing?" Momma continues.

"I guess," I say. After the park, where I saw That Girl not eat the doughnuts we brought—*what kind of name-stealing monster doesn't eat doughnuts?*—we went home to dry off and look at each other until Tom finally told the Other One it was finally time to go. Finally.

Momma reaches out and rubs my shoulders.

"You never told me—how did the board game club meeting go?"

I shrug again. "It was okay. I think a lot of people will be there today, so I'd better get going early so I can set up with Ms. Starr."

She looks at her watch. "It's really early. The library's not even open yet."

"Um, well, first I'm going over to Dad's."

"Well, honey, actually . . ."

Wait a minute. She called me honey. She's not that mad about the waffles and the bickering. Something. Is. Up.

"We, uh, need to run a little errand together, and then I'll drop you off at the library, or your dad's place, whatever you want." She's talking way too casual for this not to be something I will NOT like.

"What kind of errand?" I ask, folding my arms. "Why do I have to go? We never go on errands on Saturday mornings." Which is kind of not true, but I play it off.

Momma is making the same guilty face that Bri made that time she put all those paper towels in the toilet. "Just down to the Y. Today's the first day of . . . We thought it would be nice if . . . There's this class, well, more of a club . . ." She's mumbling! My mom is actually mumbling! This is going to be really bad.

"First day of what? I thought you said we were overscheduled already. Oh—yeah, can I sign up for ballet? Maybe, like, for a day?"

"Ballet? No. Anyway, yes, well . . . this is something new . . . and since you already take dance and swimming there, it's not really adding a whole lot. It will be fun! A workshop! And it involves digital games! Electronics! Computers!"

This is seriously suspicious. "That sounds . . . interesting," I say slowly. "You never want me to play computer games. And who's 'we'? Did you and Daddy plan this?"

"Well," she says, and she starts washing her hands again even though she just did. "It's not PLAYING them; it's making your own. Coding and stuff. It's the Girls Gaming the System Club. You love clubs! And I think your dad will be very excited too. We can tell him about it when I drop you off at his place later."

My stomach starts to hurt, and it isn't because it's sad about the waffles. It's because Momma's looking all shifty eyed, and when parents look shifty eyed, it's because they did Something for Your Own Good That You Are Not Going to Like. If she hasn't talked to Dad, then . . .

"Did you talk to *Tom* about my business, Momma?" I look at the floor. "I don't see what it has to do with him."

"Well," she says. And she takes a deep breath. "We thought it would be nice for the two of you . . . for you and his daughter . . . to do something fun. Get to know each other better." She takes another breath. "So you're going to do Girls Gaming the System. Together."

CHAPTER EIGHT

Naomi E.

I LOVE Saturday mornings! There is nothing better!

Dad and I both slept late, and now we're almost melting into the two soft blue couches with all the big pillows. We are really talented at being lazy.

Today is already feeling exactly right.

And I really needed something to be exactly right. That whole waste of a day off last Wednesday with Valerie and the other Naomi and her sister was the kind of big, shiny, awful disaster that even my dad can't ignore. I'm pretty sure he won't be forcing me to spend time with anyone else named Naomi any time soon.

Plus, the very perfect Ms. Gomez didn't give us homework

because we were awesomely great all week and no one failed the geography test. (Way to go, Luigi!)

I'm enjoying the way Dad and I are award winning at being lazy, reading, and thinking about how we'll head over to Morningstar later. The hardest thing I'm going to have to do today will be to decide between a croissant and a bagel. Poor me!

But I'm also waiting for it to be noon, because that's the time every Saturday that Mom and I are both free to Skype as long as we want. Also Wednesday afternoons, so she can hear about my week so far and what's still coming up. (But then we always end up talking other times too, because twice isn't enough. Not even close to enough.)

Which is why it makes absolutely no sense when Dad stands up and announces, "We've got to get going," at ten thirty.

I'm in my pajamas. I want to keep reading. I don't even look up. "Go where?"

Dad's in motion—the way he gets when he has to be somewhere by a certain time—moving things from here to there in a way that reminds me of a robot: keys next to door, jacket on hook, bowls in kitchen sink. "The Y," he says.

"Why?"

"The Y, yeah," he says.

Ugh, this is his favorite kind of joke, and it could go on forever; but I am not at all in the mood, because I want to sit in my pajamas until noon and then talk to my mom and then find my way with Dad to Morningstar for croissants. Or bagels.

"Get dressed, and I'll explain on the way," Dad says. He stacks sections of the *New York Times* neatly on the kitchen counter. Pushes in chairs at the table.

"What am I getting dressed for? Did I forget someone's party?" I've only ever been to the Y for birthday parties, usually swimming parties. I can't even think about the Y without feeling that sharp chlorine smell/sting in my nose that always makes me feel sick. Really sick.

"No party," Dad says. "I'll explain as we walk, but we need to get going. We'll stop by Morningstar on the way home."

"But when are we going to be *back*?" I ask, heading toward my room. "I need to be home at noon to talk to Mom."

"Do you need a sweatshirt? Don't forget your sweatshirt," Dad says. After I get dressed and washed up, we hurry out the door. "You'll have to talk to your mom later. We'll text her."

I'm feeling a little stompy about being dragged from my house until we step outside. Our neighborhood looks like the opposite of our lazy indoors Saturday. Everyone seems to be busy, doing stuff. Mr. and Mrs. Brough are pulling twigs and weeds out of the garden bed in front of their house. Two guys from the cable company are having a hard time parking at the corner. My old babysitter Jenna waves as she runs by with two pony-sized brown-and-white dogs.

"You know what's really cool?" Dad asks out of nowhere.

I keep my mouth shut. Because my dad is awesome. He is the best. He is kind and great at coming up with ideas for school projects, and he pretty much lets me eat whatever I want. But my dad and cool, I am pretty sure, have never met.

When he gets tired of waiting, he answers his own question. "Coding is cool."

The timing is perfect. Because at that exact second, Bobby Leonardo's father passes us, racing downhill on the sidewalk. On his skateboard. Bobby Leonardo's father is always on a skateboard, and it never once isn't funny, because it is the most uncool thing that could exist in the world, this old guy on a skateboard. He's good at it, I guess, but it's a fact that someone his age should not be on a skateboard. It makes my father seem maybe a tiny bit less uncool for, like, a second, by comparison.

But wait, *coding*?

Dad waves to Annie's next-door neighbor as we walk past their house. No one's home at Annie's. They're a very soccer-y family, almost always traveling for weekend games. I remember something about codes, kind of—how Annie and I used to write each other notes in this invisible ink we got at a school book fair. But it was invisible. We couldn't see a word. It wasn't that interesting.

"Why are you talking about codes?" I ask.

We're still two blocks from the Y when the sun hides behind a giant cloud. I'm glad I grabbed my sweatshirt. It gets cold. Fast.

"There's a really cool-sounding new club at the Y that I thought would be a lot of fun for you."

Since when does Dad think up ideas for me? The only reason he enrolled me in zoo camp last summer was because I begged all year. I had pictured myself as assistant zookeeper, not as someone who would walk around the zoo day after day with a big group of hot and sweaty kids. All week they talked about how on Friday we'd get to see where the monkeys sleep. I imagined something very secret and peaceful, a place where monkeys tucked themselves into beautiful, lush trees. It turned out to be a room. The monkeys sleep in a room. I learned my lesson. I don't need clubs or camps or anything to have fun.

"But I don't really care about codes. Like, at all," I say.

"It's not codes, exactly," Dad says. "It's like games, computer codes, stuff like that." We pass the bank, which has a sign that says it's 56 degrees and 10:48 a.m. It feels colder. And earlier. Dad starts walking faster, like he's racing toward something. "It's called Girls Gaming the System."

Have I mentioned that all I want is to go to Morningstar and eat a croissant? Or a bagel?

When we reach the street that the little kids call Scary Boulevard, we stop and wait for the always-takes-forever light to change. I'm about to make one more attempt to wiggle out of this when Dad says, "I know I'm repeating myself, Naomi. But this is a street only crossed when you're with an adult."

"I'm ten," I say miserably. Because ten means something so different to me than it does to him.

He's not listening anyway. "This club is all about providing opportunities," Dad said. "It meets Saturday mornings. You'll get to meet new people, make some new friends, and learn a really useful skill."

WHAT? This isn't how Dad talks. But I don't even know where to start. Saturdays are supposed to be lazy. And when am I going to talk to Mom? And I don't need new friends. "I—"

"Okay, I'll tell you what," Dad says, smiling at me. "When I pick you up, we'll go to the bakery." He holds open the door for me to walk into the Y, and that icky chlorine smell pounces before I can even think to hold my nose. Dad's looking at a form in his hand, then up at the signs on the wall, and I start walking fast too because I need to find the bathroom. I think I'm going to be sick.

CHAPTER NINE

Naomi Marie

Xiomara has a cousin who thinks she's a big deal because she's twelve and she uses Photogram even though it says right there in the rules that you have to be thirteen to post pictures. She's always bragging that it's because her parents are Progressive. I think my parents only like Progressive when it comes to schools. That gives me an idea. "I'm surprised you're making me do this," I say to Momma. "Xiomara's cousin—you know, the one you said was a little too grown—*she* probably joined a coding club, and that's why she's always posting pictures with INAPPRO-PRIATE jokes on Photogram." I glance at Momma. "At least, that's what I might have heard."

"Nice try, Naomi Marie," says Momma, pushing me gently

in the direction of the Y. Brianna skips next to us, singing a song about ice cream, which is probably what they are going to get while I'm stuck in a room with the Other One.

"Don't you care about my eyes?" I ask. "We should be thinking less screen time, not more." Since she's using my middle name, I stop there.

Momma doesn't answer as we walk inside. I slouch as much as possible on the way to Conference Room B, which is really not the name of an Interesting Place. When we get to the room, the door is closed but I can hear cheering.

"It sounds like they're having fun," Momma says, looking around. "I wonder where Tom is. . . ."

"Tom, Tom, the piper's son," sings Brianna. "Stole a pig and got some ICE CREAM!"

"That doesn't even make sense," I mumble. Momma kisses my forehead and opens the door.

There's a woman with really pretty twists standing in the front of the room. She's wearing lots of bright colors and big hoop earrings. She smiles and waves me in.

"Bye, sweetie pie!" says Momma, kissing my forehead again in front of the WHOLE ROOM.

I sit in a seat close to the door and try to look around discreetly, which is something I'm good at because Xiomara and I graduated from the spy school we started last summer. I don't see the Other Girl. Maybe she threw a tantrum and isn't coming. Because she's also a babyhead tantrum thrower.

"Welcome—I'm Julie," says the teacher. "We're just going

over a few things, then we'll get started with the DuoTek programming language. DuoTek is an awesome way to learn how to write computer code. You can create games, interactive stories, animation—anything! And it's web based, so you can work on your projects anywhere and share them with kids all over the world. In this space, we are CREATORS, not solely CONSUMERS. We are COLLABORATORS and COOPERATORS, so you'll be working in teams on a project." She's smiley, but when one of the girls in the back says "Whatever" really soft, she gives her the eye, and I can tell Julie doesn't play. She kind of reminds me of Momma, except Momma has locks.

"Sorry we're late," says a man, opening the door. It's Tom, and That Girl is slouching behind him, wrinkling her nose and holding her stomach. She glances at me, and we both nod hi quickly. She looks grouchy. Of course.

"Not at all! We're just getting going. Pickup is at one; we'll see you then!"

Tom says, "Hi, Naomi!" so I have to say "Hi" out loud back. Then he says, "Bye, Naomi!" and WE BOTH say "Bye" back! Ugh.

There are a few seats free, and one of them is right behind me. I see her looking around, and I feel like a tiny Momma is right over my shoulder, so I kind of point to it in a trying-to-be-friendly-but-not-trying-too-hard way. She sits, and I smile my smallest smile before I turn back to Julie. *Happy, Momma?*

Julie pulls up the DuoTek website on a big screen and shows us some games and stories that other kids have made, which are actually pretty cool. Some of them are adventure games, some are quiz games, a few are like a race, and one kid made a fake Hogwarts where you're supposed to have wand battles.

"Now," says Julie, "enough of me talking. Let's get to coding! Teams of two, so everyone needs to find a partner. There's an even number of you here, and I'm confident in your mature and generous spirits, so let's get to pairing up quickly and respectfully, and we'll get to work." There's that eye again.

So now there's a tiny Julie on my other shoulder, and I kind of sit there for a few seconds. Then I half turn so I can see what SHE'S doing out of the corner of my eye, and of course she's kind of sideways looking at me. It seems like everyone else partners up in about half a second, so we turn to each other and shrug.

The Other Naomi yawns so big I can see that she has a cavity. "I feel sick to my stomach. What time is it?" she whispers to me.

I move away a little and point to the clock on our computer. I wonder if it would be rude to ask if we can change partners. All the other girls look like they're about to make each other friendship bracelets any second now.

Julie claps, doing that "Okay, focus" thing teachers do when they really want to yell "BE QUIET!"

"Not only do you get the opportunity to CREATE and COOPERATE here, the DuoTek organization will be sponsoring a showcase to feature the games that demonstrate the best collaborative practices and most thoughtful content." When we all stare blankly, she translates: "The teams that work well together and produce something interesting have a chance to have their games on the DuoTek website for the whole world to see and enjoy. Capisce?"

We nod.

Julie continues, "It's open to any duo in the world who's part of a Girls Gaming the System workshop, so you'll all have the opportunity to enter. Each team will present its game during the final session, and we'll all vote on which one should represent us in the showcase." She claps again. "I'm looking forward to the magic and meaning you make over the next six weeks, ladies!"

A showcase! I can picture myself sitting at the library computers next to the Teen Gamez Crew and accidentally on purpose pulling up MY AWESOME GAME ON AN INTERNATIONAL WEBSITE. Maybe there's a medal or something, and I can wear it to school and kind of twirl it around my neck casually. *"Oh, this?"* I'll say. *"I almost forgot about it. Just a little thing I won for some programming work. It was easy, really."* But my game will be really complicated, to show that I worked hard on it. Sometimes at school it seems like no matter how many things I win, someone (like Orchid Richardson or Jenn Harlow) makes sure to *imply* that I don't really deserve it.

"Today is about DISCOVERY," says Julie. "I want you all to explore the site and play around with some basic programming. Are there any questions?"

The Other Naomi whispers, "This is going to be such a pain. I can't believe I'm here right now."

"That doesn't seem like a question," I say. "Anyway, we're stuck, so we can't just do nothing." I take out my notebook. "Let's brainstorm for the contest."

She looks around the room. "Nobody else is working, Eager Beaver. And just because my dad—" She stops.

I have plenty of experience with being called Eager Beaver (which, you know, doesn't even really rhyme), so I ignore that and point to the girls at the next computer. "Look, people *are* getting started."

She doesn't answer.

"So . . . what kinds of games do you think we can make?"

She sighs a big, heavy sigh. "Did your mom make you do this?"

I pause. "I mean, it wasn't exactly my idea." I don't add that the *most* not-my-idea part is being here with *her*. "But we might as well do the work since we're here." I wish Julie were next to us to observe how mature and generous I'm being. The Other Naomi sighs, but she stops making pukey faces and looks at the computer.

I click on "Try this NOW," and a cat called a pixie shows up. We have to use DuoTek to make her move.

"What should we name her?" says Her.

I shrug again. "I don't know. How about . . ."

"Anything but Naomi."

I look her in the eye. She's smiling.

I smile a very small smile back. "How about Eager Beaver?"

"Perfect name for a cat," she says, still smiling. I click on "Take 10 steps North" and push the mouse over to her.

She clicks on "Take 5 steps West."

We're on our way . . . somewhere.

★ ★ ★

When Julie calls, "Ten minutes," I'm actually surprised. We decide to name our cat Catastrophe, and we get the hang of using scripts to move her around pretty fast. We create a maze, and we even make her moonwalk. It's almost fun. I had no idea that programming could be like making stories. Most of the other partners are giggling and chatty, but we're quiet; I'm doing most of the work on the computer, but at least she's not making snide remarks anymore. I figure out how to add characters, and there's a ballerina with two Afro puffs like I used to wear before I got to fourth grade, where it's best to wear only one. I add her to our game.

"Do you take ballet?" she asks.

"No, West African dance," I say. "But, uh . . . I might." After a minute I ask, "What about you?"

She shakes her head, then adds, "I'm into acting, though. I'm in the drama club at my school."

"Cool," I say. I don't mention anything about drama queens or tantrums, which is pretty mature. And generous.

The Other Naomi opens her mouth, then closes it. She watches me play around with DuoTek until Julie calls time. "Congratulations on a fantastic start, ladies!" she says. "See you next week!"

Momma and Tom are standing outside the room when we come out. They both look like Brianna on Christmas morning right before she opens the biggest present.

"How was it?" they ask at the same time. Then they both laugh.

We don't. We shrug. My shoulders are getting a real workout these days.

"It was okay," I say.

"Sally go round the sunshine! Sally go round the moo-oon! Sally go round Shelly Ann's all the afternoon!" sings Brianna. Momma and Tom look at each other.

"How about some sweets?" Momma asks. "We can have Reverse Lunch today."

Ooh, dessert first! And I love Shelly Ann's! Shelly Ann's grandmother used to own it, and Shelly Ann told me that the poet Gwendolyn Brooks used to come in, order chocolate cake, and write. Some of my lists are like poems, I think. Shelly Ann lets me help take customers' orders sometimes, and she said that this year she'll teach me how to make that caramel cake.

The Other Naomi brightens up like the sun is rising from inside her. "Dad! Great idea." She turns to me. "We always go to Morningstar on Saturdays. They have the best cookies. . . . Remember the ones we brought to your house?"

"I had the hopies for Shelly Ann's!" yells Brianna.

"Morningstar sounds lovely," says Momma firmly, like she's somebody else.

"So does Shelly Ann's," adds Tom. "I can't wait to try it!"

"Dad!" says Her. "You've been there! Remember, for Annie's bake-and-take birthday party? Anyway, Morningstar—"

"Right, right," says Tom quickly. Then *he* gives *her* some side-eye. He's blushing, though. I guess she was supposed to pretend like she never heard of Shelly Ann's.

"We always go to Morningstar," she says to Momma. "My mom loved—loves—it."

I forgot that her mom moved real far away. I might be a little tantrum-y myself if I couldn't walk to Dad's anytime I want.

Momma gives her a little half smile and reaches out like she's going to pat the Other Naomi's arm, but she doesn't.

Now they're talking. Actually, now they really *are* talking, close and quiet, like people with secrets. I hate secrets that aren't mine.

I grab Brianna's hand, all big sisterly, just to let that Other Girl know. "Teach me the Sally song," I say, even though I already know it, because she sings it every five minutes.

"I'll teach everybody!" says Brianna. She starts singing, and we start walking. I think about how there will be caramel cake at Shelly Ann's. I pretend I don't notice when she puts her hand out to the Other Girl. I wonder if there's a tiny Momma on Brianna's shoulder too or if she just doesn't know any better. Or maybe she's following my example, like a little sister should. Something almost like the hopies flutters in my belly. Maybe Shelly Ann's caramel cake will be magic and make the Other Naomi nice. And then she'll go home and be nice there, where I won't have to see it but I'll know I helped. Maybe if I keep being so mature, I can make all this go away and then I can be myself again. The one and only Naomi.

CHAPTER TEN

Naomi E.

The little one, Brianna, reaches out to hold my hand, and before I even know it, the other Naomi and I are swinging her the way Mom and Dad used to swing me on my way to Kinder Kinder (which almost rhymes with *finder splinter*, but everyone calls it Kinda Kinder) when I was little. It's weird to be the older one, the big one. I've never been the one who swings before. It's fun, but only for about a minute. And it seems like Brianna would like us to keep swinging her until our arms fall off our bodies.

And she won't stop singing!

Everyone else is pretending it's adorable. The other Naomi sometimes chimes in—in harmony. Dad might even be— Yes, he is. Dad is singing along.

We turn left at the corner instead of going straight, the direction of Morningstar. "Dad!" I call out. He and Valerie got far ahead of us because they don't have to swing a four-year-old.

He turns and smiles.

"Dad, Morningstar's that way," I remind him.

Valerie, who I wasn't talking to, answers. "We thought it would be fun to try someplace new."

"Shelly Ann's?" the other Naomi says. "I think we might *really* need her caramel cake today."

"Today we're trying Yumi's," Valerie says. "It opened two weeks ago."

I'm not going to act like a brat, but I feel like one inside. Because all I want is to be at Morningstar. I kind of *need* the way everyone smiles at Dad and me when we walk in. And the table in the corner that's almost always waiting for us. Plus a bagel. Or a croissant. It's almost like our home away from home, especially since Mom left.

I stop swinging my arm, but Brianna pulls my hand back, trying to force another swing. The other Naomi and I do one more quick swing and then I drop Brianna's hand before she can try for more. We've been swinging her for two whole blocks already!

"Everything's good at Shelly Ann's," Brianna sings in the same way she was singing that "Sally Go Round" song, but the words don't fit the melody. "We'll go there next time because it's the best bakery in the wor-er-er-erld!"

"You're something else, Brianna," Dad says, laughing.

Finally, we stop in front of a storefront with a little blackboard easel sign out front that says Open for Business. It's new looking and cute, and when we open the door, a delicious buttery-cinnamon-apple smell greets us. There's something about it—Oh. Ow, oh. It smells like the apple crisp my mom makes. She says it's the one recipe she's never messed up, and it makes me miss her in a really big way. Shoot, my eyes are tearing up and everything. From a stupid smell!

"Dad," I whisper, "do you think there's a bathroom here?" I don't want to cry in front of everyone.

"It may be only for the people who work here, but I can ask."

"Naomi! LOOK!" Brianna runs over to the display case. "They have the biggest cookies! That one is bigger than Rahel!"

A bald guy who's lining up cupcakes on a low shelf stands up. Whoa. He's very tall, and his smile somehow makes me feel better. I wipe my eyes with the back of my hand, relieved no one saw.

"What can I get for you?" he asks.

"Your bathroom?" Valerie asks.

I always forget that I'm a lousy whisperer.

"I'm okay," I say. "Thanks." I smile at her. Dad looks so proud that I have to look away.

Which isn't hard, because I'm in a bakery! Cookies with sprinkles, black-and-white cookies, chocolate chip, oatmeal chip, five kinds of cupcakes, brownies, blondies.

Brianna's putting her fingers all over the display case, making marks—something I feel like I was born knowing not to do.

"Are you going to have a bagel or a croissant?" Dad asks me.

"We don't sell bagels," the bald guy says. "Can I get you a croissant?"

I see them in a little basket. They don't look all buttery and delicious.

"Could you tell me what's making that smell? That, like, apple-y–cinnamon thing. Is it a crisp or a tart or—"

"Our famous sunny-apple-morning muffin."

"Muffins are cake shaped like breakfast!" Brianna says.

"Can I get you one?" the man asks.

Before Brianna can start singing about a muffin man, I blurt, "Sure. A muffin sounds great." I regret it right away. A muffin? I ordered a muffin?

The other Naomi makes a face like I ordered stewed turtle or something.

The man—is he Yumi?—puts the muffin on a plate, and I take it to a table with four seats. The table wobbles when I put my plate on it, so I stand to move to another but not before Valerie sits next to me. "Tell me what you thought of the club," she says. "Did you have fun?"

Over her shoulder, I can see the other Naomi and Brianna pointing at brownies and cookies. Desserts! And I'm eating a stupid breakfast muffin. A muffin's better than, I don't know, toast. But it's definitely not cake shaped like breakfast. Which is wrong anyway, Brianna. It's breakfast shaped like a cupcake. Why didn't I get a cookie?

"Well, I didn't know anything about DuoTek before the class, so I definitely learned stuff. The teacher, Julie, was nice. It was okay, I guess." But it wasn't about liking or not liking the class. It was about *not* liking being tricked into doing it. I didn't like that at all, and I know I have to wait until Dad and I are alone before I tell him. For now, though, I have to eat a stupid muffin. On a wobbly table.

The tables at Morningstar don't wobble.

Brianna races toward the table and nearly breaks her plate when she slams it down. "I call I get to sit between the Naomis. Naomi, you sit there," she says, pointing at her sister and then at the chair on her other side.

The other Naomi takes a deep breath. "I will sit where I want to sit, Brianna." Then she sneaks a look at her mom and sits in the chair Brianna is pointing at.

"Want anything, Val?" Dad calls from the counter. "Maybe split a doughnut?"

Who splits doughnuts? Dad could eat three doughnuts in one sitting, easy.

Valerie has the same idea. "Why split? Let's get two and share."

He comes to the table with one chocolate doughnut and one jelly. Valerie stands and offers Dad her seat.

"Val, please sit," Dad says. "I'm happy to stand."

"So am I," she says.

Neither of them sits.

"What did you get?" I ask the other Naomi.

"I got a butterscotch cookie," Brianna says.

"She was talking to me," the other Naomi says, but she says it in a calm voice. One that sounds used to an interrupting little kid. "I was going to get caramel cake. But this place doesn't have that, so I got a triple-chocolate cookie."

"Triple?" I say. "What's the third?"

Brianna starts singing something about triple being the most chocolate. Naomi talks over her. "There's the cookie, the chips, and then there's chocolate frosting on top. Want to try it?"

I shake my head.

We're all quiet. I pull the top off my stupid muffin and eat it, trying not to think about all the better things I could be eating.

"So, Naomi, tell us about Girls Gaming the System," Dad says.

I don't say anything, because I already told Valerie. And Dad and I can talk about it for real later, when we're home. But the silence grows, so finally I say, "It was fine," at the exact same time the other Naomi says, "It was okay."

Brianna cracks up. And doesn't stop.

"I'm going to get some tea," Valerie says, walking to the counter. "Does anyone else want anything?"

I want to trade in my tastes-nothing-like-my-mother's-apple-crisp muffin for a triple-chocolate cookie, but I'm too embarrassed to ask.

"I'll have a cup of coffee," Dad says. "I need to dunk this in something," he says, holding up the tiny bit of doughnut he has left.

"You two Naomis always think everyone's talking to you," Brianna says, looking at her sister and then at me. She's still staring at me when she asks, "Do you have a middle name?"

I feel myself blushing. I don't like talking about middle names. Because I hate mine. Well, I love the *reason* for my name. I'm named after one of the most famous costume designers of all time because Mom is obsessed with her. This woman won eight Academy Awards! EIGHT! And she was brilliant, but unfortunately, her name was not Ruby Head. Or Violet Head. Or Anything-Other-than-Edith Head.

I'm Naomi Edith.

Which Dad knows I like to keep secret. So it's hard to know why he blurts it out right as Valerie's coming back to the table with two mugs in her hands.

"She's Naomi Edith. And you're Naomi Marie, right?" Dad asks.

I open my mouth to object and to ask how he already knows the other Naomi's middle name. But I don't want to make it even worse in front of this whole other family. What's he going to do next? Talk about the time I threw up on the escalator when he took me to see the Harlem Globetrotters?

"EDITH?" Brianna says, way too loudly.

"I think it's a nice name," Valerie says.

"It's for a costume designer," I say. "She designed those gorgeous clothes Audrey Hepburn wore in *Roman Holiday* and *Sabrina*."

Valerie nods. "Edith Head," she says. Which is really surprising, because hardly anyone has ever heard of her.

"That's cool," the other Naomi says. Then she looks at my plate. "Don't you like your muffin?"

"I'm not that hungry," I say.

She smiles and hands me a piece of her cookie. Which is the most delicious thing I ever ate.

And I decide right then that I'm going to try to be Kinda Kinder.

CHAPTER ELEVEN

Naomi Marie

I'm acting like I'm cool with this whole Momma-and-Tom thing. I have to admit, it's making Momma more free and easy, like when she lets Xiomara come over for a playdate during the week, and she lets us watch TV so we settle in for *Vocalympians!*, which is not so much a perk because A LOT OF PEOPLE CAN'T SING and also Brianna thinks it's a sing-along show; but we laugh and pretend to have our own show anyway. Even doing homework together is fun, and I feel a teeny-tiny bit like it's okay for *some* things to change. But I'm not saying that out loud.

"You should sign up for this DuoTek workshop," I say to Xiomara. "Then we could be partners."

"I thought the whole idea was for you to be partners with the Other Naomi," she says.

"Yeah," I say. She was almost okay at that bakery, which I might possibly go to again, because that cookie was good. "But I can tell she's not going to take it that seriously; she mostly looks bored while she watches me do the work. I don't want the teacher to think I'm a slacker."

"And I thought you didn't even want to do it," says Xiomara.

"I didn't," I answer. "But now that I am, I want it to be good. There's even a showcase! Remember when we had to work in groups for our Lenape projects? And Jenn Harlow and Orchid Richardson didn't do anything, so I finished their wampum belts for them? And Mr. Mack assumed that they had done all the work because Orchid went on and on about how she'd gone to the American Indian museum over the weekend, *and* she brought Mr. Mack a frybread mix? Talk about fake."

"Yeah, I remember. You bring it up a lot. You should have told your mom," says Xiomara.

I never tell Momma about school stuff, because it would get too weird. I try not to act all like MY MOMMA WORKS HERE, because sometimes the kids say that I only get check pluses because my mom is a librarian and probably does all my work. They're the ones who think that I'm not that smart and that I know every hip-hop dance. I know for a fact that Jenn's mom is a Rich Person and hires people to do Jenn's work. But nobody cares about that.

"You should have us both sleep over next weekend," says

Xiomara, smoothing the stickers on her science folder.

"You and *Jenn*?" I ask, confused. "Um, are you feeling okay?"

"No, duh, me and the Other Naomi. That would be fun. Can she sing? I wrote a new song, and we could be like a trio. What did you say her middle name was again? Agatha?"

"Er, no, it's Edith," I say. I'm not sure I was supposed to tell that. Well, okay, I'm pretty sure I wasn't. "She's named after a famous costume designer, and actually she does dress pretty nice." There, that makes it better. "But I don't know if she can sing."

"That's okay; you can't either," says Xiomara, giggling. I throw my LOVE pillow at her as Brianna barges in.

"Can I play?" she asks. "It's my room too, and privacy's not fair."

"MOMMA!" I call.

Brianna runs out of the room, and I close the door behind her, a tiny bit hard but not a real slam. She's always trying to break the Playdate Privacy Rule. I get one sister-free hour in here, and I'm using every minute of it.

"Let's play Life," Xiomara says. "Kwame never plays with me." Xiomara's brother, Kwame, used to be so nice; but now that he's thirteen he burps, sweats, and ignores me.

We set up the board. "A sleepover wouldn't work. Brianna would be in our faces the whole time, and she's an only child, so she wouldn't get it."

"I know! We could go to your dad's!" says Xiomara.

"Come on," I say. "I can't bring *her* to my *dad's*. That would be . . . so rude." Xiomara claps a hand over her mouth. "I'm so sorry! I forgot who she is! Are you mad at me?"

YES is what I want to shout. "That's okay," I say, but it's not. "Anyway, I already spend Saturday mornings with her, I don't know if I want to do a sleepover too. She looks like she snores." And just like that, all the fun is sucked out of the day, like I'm still sitting in the tub after the bubble bath has drained out. "I don't want to play Life; it's boring."

Xiomara's looking at me like she's about to cry, and I know she feels bad, but I don't say anything; I just put all the game pieces back in the box. Then I yell, "Briaannna! You can come play!" and open the door. She's sitting right there, with her Rahel doll and purse full of Country Corner Critters.

"YAY!!!" She rolls into the room. "Can you braid Rahel's hair?"

"Yeah," I answer. "Cornrows again?" Brianna nods. Xiomara stands up slowly.

"Well, I guess I should go. . . ."

"Okay, bye," I say. Then I look up. "I'll walk you to the door."

Momma gives Xiomara some brownies to take home to Kwame.

"Do you want to do homework at the library tomorrow?" Xiomara asks.

I look away. "Sure," I say.

"I'm *really* sorry," she says again.

"I know, it's fine," I say, and I give her a hug plus our special best-friends hand squeeze.

"NAOMI!" shouts Brianna from the bedroom. "I made a braid myself!"

"You and your sister need to start getting ready for bed," says Momma after I say good-bye to Xiomara and close the door.

"Can we have banana splits first?" I ask. Momma looks at me. "Worth a try," I say, and I give her a hug too.

"You know, I was thinking," she starts. "Why don't we have Tom's daughter, Naomi, come over here next weekend after your workshop. Maybe she can even sleep over. That might be fun."

Oh my goodness, MOMMA'S MAGIC. I knew it.

"Were you eavesdropping?" I ask. "Because that's not cool, Momma."

"No, I wasn't. I've been thinking about it, but as you well know, I am not concerned with being cool, and you shouldn't be either. I hope that if there was something important going on, you would talk to me about it—and why do you ask that anyway? Were you girls talking about having her over? That's wonderful, Naomi Marie. I'm so glad. I *knew* you would warm up!"

Did she even take a breath? And what's with calling me Naomi Marie? Is she mad, sad, glad, or what?

"Um, I'm still kind of cold, Momma," I say. "I mean, she seems okay and all, but why so much togetherness? It's not like we have to be play cousins or something. I mean, Tom's okay, but . . . he's not my dad."

She touches my cheek and leads me to the couch; I don't even see her wince when I sit on her lap. I lean all the way back onto her, like I'm little again.

"Going to the library tomorrow?" she asks. "What do you and Ms. Starr have planned next?"

"We had talked about a Sequence tournament. But since I can't do the board game club anymore . . . ," I say, leaning back on her.

"Oh, honey, I know Girls Gaming the System changed that." She hugs me a little tighter. "Maybe you could do something with board games on Saturday afternoons instead?"

"I'll ask Dad," I say. "He'll understand." I'm not sure if she heard me put a little extra attitude in there, but she doesn't say anything. We had the word *disrupt* on the vocabulary test last week, and it feels like that word has moved into my life for good. I think about the last time I was at Dad's. We were playing Sequence, and I was winning until Brianna spread the pieces all over the board and messed it up. Dad and I made up a whole new game and built a tower with the pieces. We laughed, but I was also still a little mad that we never really finished the game.

"Ms. Starr said we're going to have to try something else anyway, since . . . um, not that many people seem interested. Miyuri and I thought about a current events book club; she watches *Newshour* with her parents too. But then we'd have to pick sad books, and they just make you feel worse." Last night, I started listing every time Gwen Ifill mentioned racism, guns, poor people, angry people, sick people, wars . . . and then I stopped writing.

"I agree that the news these days is pretty depressing," Momma says. "But sometimes sad stories help something good grow out of the sadness—they illuminate," she says. "And remember the news stories about Johari Osayi Idusuyi?" She smiles. "She *literally* used a book to make something good out of a very sad situation. You guys can turn your sadness into action."

I smile too. "Ha, that's true. . . . Thanks, Momma."

". . . And maybe after you and Tom's Naomi finish this workshop, you guys can start a coding club at the library."

"There's already Teen Gamez Crew," I say. "And she doesn't go to our library."

"Well . . . think about it. I bet Ms. Starr would be interested."

I picture myself doing a DuoTek demonstration for the Teen Gamez Crew. Their mouths are hanging open, and I smile and pretend not to notice. That would be cool.

"Maybe I'll show Dad what I'm learning," I say.

"And they don't live that far away, Tom and his daughter," she continues, like I never said anything. "I bet she'd like to meet Ms. Starr."

Back to that again. That girl is going to take over my whole life if I'm not careful!

"That would be weird, Momma" is all I say.

"Well . . . think about it. And you could introduce Xiomara too. Maybe the three of you can have a playdate."

If Momma *is* magic, it's not the good kind that gives you your heart's desire.

And that *Naomi Marie*'s still bugging me.

"Why did you call me *Naomi Marie* just now? I'm not in trouble, am I?"

"What do you mean? Of course you're not in trouble."

"Well, usually you say that when you're mad."

"I don't *always* do that. And I don't get mad . . . I get *concerned*," says Momma. "Sometimes *deeply* concerned." She smiles and pokes me. "Anyway, I don't know. I guess now that there are two Naomis in my life, that's how I think of *you*. My own special Naomi Marie."

I used to just be special as Naomi, though.

Brianna comes into the living room, holding up Rahel. "I did it!" she says. Rahel has some lumpy-looking knots in her hair that look like they'll never come out. And she's sporting my blue-and-purple butterfly clip.

"She looks beautiful," I say. I look at Momma, and we both push back a laugh. I move over. "You can sit on Momma's other leg if you want."

Momma hugs us both to her. "You girls are growing up! Sometimes I wish I could freeze you in time."

That's what I'm trying to tell you, Momma. Just keep things like they are. Stop moving the pieces all over the board!

Momma looks at her watch. "Oh, how about a banana split?" she asks.

"Yay!" yells Brianna. She jumps up and down, and I hug her for no reason except that she's my sister and she's little and she's happy and she doesn't understand everything.

I want to cheer too, but something gets caught in my throat. A banana split dinner is supposed to mean a celebration. I think I'd feel better if Momma just made us go to bed.

CHAPTER TWELVE

Naomi E.

"The no-head ladies got there!" I say when Mom's face appears on the computer. They're behind her. I'd say they were looking at her, except that no *heads* means no *eyes*.

She looks confused for a second—she doesn't call them that. "Oh! Yeah. The box got here on Thursday," she says. "Thank you for sending it."

I try to notice details about the room she's in, but all I can see is that the walls are pale yellow, and there's a lamp behind a flowery chair in the corner. It is so impossible and weird that she's living in a place I've never seen.

"Are you working all the time?" I ask. That's what she said

it would be like in California. When she lived here, she did costumes mostly for plays, and it was crazy for a month or two and
then she'd have lots of time to do stuff with me. But this job is
lasting longer. She didn't know what it would be like when she
first went there, but she's really good and people keep offering
her new jobs. Right now, she's working on a movie, but she said
she might be starting on a TV show as soon as the movie's over.

She smiles at me. Well, at the camera. But at me. "It feels
like it, yeah. So tell me about this class that changed our talks to
Sundays. Or is it a club? I wasn't clear—"

"It's this coding class at the Y. DuoTek? Making computer
games and stuff. Dad calls it a club, but it's just a class."

She's quiet for a minute, looking at my face on the screen.
"Interesting," she says.

And then she does this thing that I somehow almost forgot
about. She says the exact opposite of the truth with a very straight
face. "You've been a student of computer science for a very long
time." She nods, looking very serious. "If I recall correctly, your
interest began when you were three months old."

I picture myself dressed in a onesie, a baby bottle by my side,
pounding on a keyboard, and it makes me laugh.

It used to drive Dad crazy when we talked like this. He always
thought there was a little meanness in it. But he gives me privacy
when I Skype with Mom, so I don't worry about him overhearing.
"I begged Dad to sign me up because computer games are my
passion!" It's funny, because I never play computer games.

She laughs, but there's a question in it.

"Why *are* you doing it?"

I think of a truth that won't hurt her, because I don't know if Mom knows about Valerie. "Dad's friend's daughter is in the class. And he really wants us to be friends."

"Do you like her? Is she fun?" It reminds me of the way Mom and I used to talk at the kitchen table, the way she was curious about everything that happened to me, where Dad seems fine with whatever I tell him.

I try to find the right words. Does Mom even know I'm talking about Dad's *female* friend's daughter? But I say, "It's a six-week class," which doesn't answer her question at all.

"Listen," she says. "Sometimes I'm stuck with people I wouldn't choose to work with. Remember Joshua, the production designer on *Pilgrims' Pets: The Musical?*"

"Yeah, I think. He was super-bossy, right?"

"Well, there was a lot going on, but yeah, you could say that. But I thought about that interview with Edith Head we watched, and it really helped. Do you remember?"

"The one that showed Audrey Hepburn?" She was so beautiful.

"Yes. And Edith talked about how she starts each new project. She said something like 'The first thing I do is get to know the actress. I actually study her.'"

I think about the way Mom reads and rereads a script before she begins designing. "Wait, don't you mean the character she's playing? Not the actress?"

"That's what made Edith Head different. She would study

the actress, see how she stood, walked, moved. To learn as much as she could."

"So you think I should study her? To learn . . . what? I mean, why?"

"It's a way of getting to know someone. To think about it from a different angle, or a few angles. The way a director might."

All of a sudden, I'm hit with a wave of missing Mom. "Do you know when you're coming home?" I ask.

She nods, and I feel so much hope. But then she says, "I need to talk to your dad about some things."

"Okay," I say. And then I say, "He's very organized. I keep him in charge of my schedule because he's so organized."

We both laugh again.

"I miss you like nobody's business," Mom says.

Don't cry.

"I need to see you soon, Mom," I say. "This is too long, it's been too long, and it's too hard," and then, shoot! I start to cry.

Mom's eyes tear up a little too. "I'm going to talk to your dad. I was thinking maybe it'll be better if you come out here for the first visit."

Is that hope or excitement or something else that flips like an in-my-stomach seal? "Really?"

"Not right away, but yes. When you have no school and I have some time off."

I'm still hurting from missing her, but the tears stop. A trip to California sounds perfect! I could escape that stupid Girls Gaming the System class AND see my mom.

"Do you want to talk to him now?" I ask, ready to run and get him and the school calendar so it can all happen this exact instant.

But Mom says, "I have to go now. I have some sketches I need to finish, and I need to meet with my team, but—"

"On a Sunday?" I say.

"On an every day. I know. It's crazy. But I'll talk to your dad during the week. We'll figure this out, Naomi." She smiles and blows me a kiss.

"I love you," I say, and then the screen closes.

After I talk to Mom, I usually feel the way I do after a good meal, like the conversation is all I need to fill me all the way with her love. Once I tell her what's going on in my life and hear about hers, it's like everything's okay. But today it feels like there are holes, and the stuff that keeps me feeling like me is spilling out a little. Part of it is I'm mad at my dad, and also I don't know when I'm going to see my mom. It's too much, and it's too hard. I picture the way most of the pellet-y stuffing came out of Lambikins when Mom put her in the washing machine when I was four.

Dad sticks his head into the room. "Good. You're off. I was hoping you could show me some of what you learned yesterday. I don't know the first thing about DuoTek."

I'm not sure what I want to do right now, but I know it's not that. I don't even want to think about that class right now. And then I realize what's been missing from this weekend—an easy thing to do that might make me feel a little more normal. "Can we go to Morningstar?" I ask. I can almost picture the croissant I'll eat. Or the bagel.

"I thought maybe we could do that next week," Dad says. "With Valerie and her girls, after we get you at the Y."

"I don't want to sound mean, Dad, but can't we ever do anything with just the two of us anymore?"

"Don't you like them?" he asks. There's a sadness in his face that I haven't seen since those long, hard months when he and Mom went through that awful separation.

"Can't we do both? Go now and then go again next week?"

"I'm not that hungry," he says. I forgot how small his voice sounded then. Like it sounds now. "Are you?"

It's not about hungry. It's about wanting to do what we do. About wanting to go to Morningstar with just my dad. But I can't stand to see him like this.

What I really want to say is "Of course, Dad. I don't want a delicious buttery croissant one bit! All I want is to show you what I learned to do with your girlfriend's daughter. Who stole my name. I've always hated croissants! And bagels."

But like I said, Dad does not find the way Mom and I talk funny. And he looks so sad. So instead I show him how to move a cat around a screen. And try to remember why I was going to be nicer to the other Naomi.

But I know the answer. Not only did I feel bad that she has an annoying little sister, but I almost like her. She's super-smart. But I really don't like the way Dad's pushing me toward her.

At all.

CHAPTER THIRTEEN

Naomi Marie

"This town ain't big enough for the both of you," Tom says in a fake-growly voice, and everybody groans, even the Other One.

Momma frowns at him. *Now?* she mouths, like all of us can't lip-read a word like *now*. Come on, parents.

"What Tom means," says Momma slowly, "is that we should talk about our . . . name situation."

"Do we really have to talk about this now, right before we go in?" asks the Other Naomi, and I nod because, *Come on*, parents! At least *someone* understands. If I didn't have to take this class with her and she wasn't who she was and she wasn't already trying to steal my life starting with MY NAME, I might invite her to visit my book review club at the library. As a one-time guest.

Right now, I don't want to work anything out except our project. This week we're finishing up this really cool minigame that's based on old arcade games like pinball. Then we want to make a trivia game, with questions about our favorite books. Actually, her taste in books is pretty good. The cool thing about DuoTek is that we can each see when the other person updates the project. On Monday, I saw that she listed *The Trouble with Half a Moon* and *Breadcrumbs* in the Brain Dump section. So I added a sticky note that said, "Cool!! I love those books too!!!" I spent a long time deciding how many exclamation points to add, and I put in a smiley face, but the one that doesn't show teeth because I thought she might think the teeth one is stupid. But she never responded. I checked every day when I added ideas to the Dump.

"Work it out, Two Naomis, work it out!" sings Bri, dancing in a circle.

"Well, we can, um, work this out quickly—Tom and I already have an idea," Momma says, and then I realize that they must have planned this, just like this, so we wouldn't have time to think. Again: Come *on*, parents!

"Since we have this coincidence here, with both of you named Naomi and all," starts Tom.

"We thought that one of you could use your middle name," finishes Momma. Then she looks straight at me.

Wait, what? "What are you looking at me for?" I ask loudly. I point to the Other One. "*She's* got a middle name too. A perfectly . . . uh, actual one." I don't want to make fun of her name because that's not cool, even if she is obviously kind of embarrassed about it. And I mean: Edith. That's kind of old school, like one of those shows Nana likes. Some people in my school would probably have a lot to say about it, like Mikey, who always has some annoying comment to make. I sneak a quick glance her way. She's not looking at me, but I learned last Saturday that when she gets mad, she bites her lip kind of hard, and she's about to draw blood right now.

Momma and Tom look at each other. "Please, honey," Momma says. "It will just . . . make things easier."

What would make things easier is if my parents could have made it work like they always want us kids to do, and if Tom wasn't kind of nice even though he's the Enemy, and if the Other One didn't have a secret middle name that she maybe hated and I didn't get called Naomi Marie when Momma's mad, and if I could just be at the library with Xiomara and Ms. Starr and play games with my dad and Brianna could have extended days at school.

"But you only call me Naomi Marie when I'm in trouble!" I say. "I'm going to always feel like you're mad at me!"

I am NOT going to cry.

Momma hugs me, but I squirm away. Brianna stops singing and holds my hand.

"Oh honey—you're right. Let's talk about this later," Momma says. "I didn't realize . . . Well, we just thought . . ."

"It's my fault," said Tom, which, DUH! YES I KNOW THAT. "And you're absolutely right. Talking about something like this right before you go in probably isn't a good time."

I look away from them both, until the Other One says, "But maybe we do need to work something out, Dad, because *I'm* the one who said that about it being right before we go in. I guess it's soooo hard for you to tell us apart!"

I was wrong. She doesn't bite her lip when she's mad; she gets really red. Really. But the idea of anyone not being able to tell us apart is kind of . . . funny. Before I realize it, I let out a giggle.

She looks straight at me. And grins.

We don't talk about it at all. We both know it's weird, and there's too much to do anyway. And I'm doing most of it. As usual. But I don't mind so much, because this is actually more fun than I'd expected, thinking of ways to make a digital game that's exciting like a real game. And this time the Other Naomi doesn't just watch; even though I still do all the work on the computer, she seems interested in my ideas for a book trivia adventure game, and we find out that we both had to read *The Great Wall of Lucy Wu* for school and we agree that it was AWESOME.

As we're packing up, she says, "So . . . they'll be back soon. What's our plan?"

"Plan?" I ask. "Um." I'm not sure what to say. We look at each other for a minute; then I add, "Parents always do stuff like that. They think they can just trick us into doing what they want."

"I know," she says. "My best friend Annie's mom asked her to sing in front of everyone at Thanksgiving dinner last year. The whole family was there, even her cousins who are teenagers. Her mom blurted it out right after she told Annie that she could have an extra slice of pie instead of Brussels sprouts. Annie almost died. Literally."

"Whoa!" I say. "Wait till I tell Xiomara that one, though she probably would have whipped out her personal microphone and spotlight. She's obsessed with *Vocalympians!*"

"Who's Xiomara?"

"She's *my* best friend," I say.

"Oh. Well, so do you think we should present a, um . . . united front?"

I pause. "I guess so. But . . . well." I stop.

"I know. It's . . . your name."

"Yeah . . . yours too," I say. "It's cool that you're named after that lady. Are, um, your parents really into costumes?" I wonder if they all dress up for Halloween.

"My mom is a costume designer," she says, not looking at me. "She's working on a big movie, with lots of stars. In California." She closes her mouth like she's never going to open it again.

I wonder what it's like to have your mom so far away. I wonder how I would feel if my dad wasn't right down the street. I wonder if all this wondering is going to make things even more complicated.

I can see Momma and Tom outside the door. "Okay, the plan . . . ," I say. "The plan is . . . I'm not sure yet. But, look . . ." I nod toward Momma's and Tom's big smiles and waves. They're practically jumping up and down.

We look at each other and sigh.

"Here's an idea. . . . We thought we could all go to the beach!" says Momma as we walk out to the sidewalk.

"It's not summer," the Other Naomi says, which is both a good point and also *Shhh, Other Naomi! They said we're going to the beach!* But then she says to her father, "And since when do you like the beach?"

"We thought we'd try something that would be fun for all of us," Tom says. "A little celebration to, uh, thank you both for being so mature, and . . ." He trails off.

"Nobody agreed to anything yet," says the Other Naomi, and I'm glad she said it and not me. She's giving her father some kind of stare. I wonder what that's all about.

"What about me?" asks Brianna. "I was line leader yesterday. Mrs. Cullen says I'm very mature!"

I roll my eyes, but I don't say anything.

"Let's just celebrate all of us being mature!" says Momma, and she and Tom look at each other, all happy. I look away—right at the Other Naomi. I can tell she sees the big, hopeful smiles too. We look at each other and that mad-at-her-father thing melts, and we smile too. Small smiles. But even though they're small, they're real. Because, parents.

CHAPTER FOURTEEN

Naomi E.

When I used to go to the beach with Mom and Dad, we'd get a car and drive out to Jones Beach on Long Island, which is the best. There are these huge parking lots, and sometimes you walk through tunnels where your voice echoes over and over and it all smells like rainbow sherbet. Mom always said it reminded her of when she was a girl, and it made her happy. And that made me happy.

But it never made my dad happy. Going to the beach actually made him miserable. He always complained about the sand coming home with us, how long the drive was, everything! And yet here we all are, on the subway, going to the beach, and Dad's all smiley. There's only one seat, and Valerie takes it and pulls Brianna onto her lap, so Naomi and I grip a pole on either side of my dad.

"It was supposed to be a beautiful day," Valerie says, looking out at the gray sky when the subway comes out of the tunnel.

"It was," Dad says. "But it'll be fun, because we're all together." Really?

"I'm going to build fourteen castles and be the ruler of them all," Brianna sings. The people sitting near them smile at her and then at Valerie. An old lady with a thick accent—Russian or German or something—says to Valerie, "She is absolutely precious." Valerie smiles, and Brianna sits up tall and straight, like a super-proud bird or a statue.

I switch from holding the pole with my right hand to my left so I can turn and face away from them.

At the last stop, we get off the train, and Dad takes the two bags Valerie's carrying and puts one over each of his shoulders.

I remind Dad how much I love the boardwalk, which is the only good thing about going to the beach in Brooklyn.

"I went with Xiomara last summer, and her brother, Kwame, won three basketballs," the other Naomi says.

"Did he give you one?"

"Of course not," she says. "But then when we got soft-serve ice cream, he got green. Green! It's pistachio, I think, but who chooses green?"

"Good question," I say. "Dad, can we maybe do the board-walk too, because it's a little cold but not too cold for walking and definitely not too cold for ice cream and—"

"Naomi, not today." The voice he keeps using with me is not one of my favorites. I can tell I'm getting on his nerves. I wonder if he knows he's kind of getting on mine too. Last night when I asked him if he had talked to Mom about when I could go to California, he complained to me about leaving messages for Mom and missing calls like it was all my fault. I just want to see my mom!

Once we reach the beach, it feels so weird to slide off my shoes and socks and put my feet in the not-at-all-warm-like-it-usually-is-when-I'm-at-the-beach sand. It smells like beach, like, I don't know, maybe seagulls.

Brianna drops to her knees and starts digging with her hands. "Hold on, Brianna," Valerie calls. "We have blankets. And once we're all set up, I have shovels and pails. Just slow down."

Brianna lets out a big sigh and flops down on her butt. "Fine, I'll wait," she says.

Valerie hands the other Naomi a big colorful blanket and says, "Can you and Naomi lay this neatly on the ground?"

We each take two corners and spread the blanket out in the air. It's a beautiful blanket, blue and green, and like pretty fabrics always do, it makes me think of my mother. I remember what she said about Edith Head, how she studied people to get to know them. I watch Naomi as we slowly lower the blanket to the sand. She reminds me of a teacher. The way she stands with her back so straight. Maybe *confident* is the right word. Edith Head would make the other Naomi confident costumes, for sure.

Before we even finish smoothing the blanket out, Brianna

throws herself on it, getting sand all over everything and making the blanket wrinkly and messy. "I call that this is *my* blanket, and you can sit on it if you help me. I'm building fourteen castles, and I might need help with the goats and—"

"Goats?" I ask. "Your castle has goats?" She doesn't know this, but I LOVE goats. Especially baby goats. A castle with goats sounds interesting. . . .

Brianna rolls her eyes at me in a way I've seen the other Naomi roll her eyes. "Every castle has goats. It's like a big swimming pool that goes around the castle with goats swimming in it."

The other Naomi shakes her head. "It's a moat. I've told you. Moat. Not goat."

"Well, I'm going to need water, so where are the pails for getting water?"

Valerie smiles but doesn't look happy. "Why don't we sit here for a while? Maybe eat a little something. Before you run off, Brianna, I thought we could all sit and talk—"

"Could I please have a shovel? I need to start. Fourteen's a lot of castles."

"Come on, Brianna," Dad says. "Let's go get some water. I know you have a lot of work to do. Fourteen *is* a lot of castles."

I watch as Dad, holding Brianna's hand, walks toward the ocean. I'm trying to not think about how not-nice-about-going-to-the-beach he always was. A lot of times Mom and I went without him.

I wish I could stop looking, but I can't.

If I studied Brianna to create a costume for her, it would be every loud color, and it would have arms and antennas reaching in every direction like a sea witch. Or a bright storm-cloud octopus.

I'm so grateful when Valerie asks if I want a cupcake, because yes, I do. And it helps me pull my eyes away from Dad and Brianna. As Valerie's reaching for the box, I notice that the other Naomi is busy writing something in a little notebook. She sees me staring and puts the notebook down and slides her leg over it.

Maybe she's been studying me just like I've been studying her.

She looks like she got caught doing something wrong, and I can almost see her brain thinking of something to say. "So, what do you think about that project?" she asks.

"What project?"

"The one Julie talked about. Remember? She said now that we know how to use DuoTek, we can start creating our game. And the best one will be in that contest?"

I look in the cupcake box. I do not want to end up with disguised coconut again, so I take a chocolate-chocolate one. Can't go wrong with that.

"Solid choice," the other Naomi says. "I'm having this one. It looks like vanilla, but I'm pretty sure the cake is coconut."

I knew it.

"It's delicious," she says, "and I can't believe I'm getting it before Brianna, because she—" And then she stops talking.

I see why. Dad and Brianna are walking toward us, looking like great buddies, each carrying a bucket with water. Brianna's water is sloshing out of the bucket, and she's already wet. Dad is smiling and asks, "And where should I put it, your Royal

Highness? Where will you be building your fourteen castles, m'lady?"

I turn back to the other Naomi. "Is that what you were writing down in your notebook?" I ask. "Stuff about the DuoTek project?" She seems really into our class, like maybe she'll grow up to be a woman gaming the system.

"No. I was working on a list. I . . . write a lot of lists."

"What about?" Maybe I was right! She *is* studying me!

"We have the Geo Challenge at school this week, and I want to remember to get some books at the library."

Brianna plops down between the other Naomi and me and starts digging.

"Why do you have to do that right here, Brianna?'

"To make it easy for you to help me." She turns to me. "And you too."

Two little boys and their parents walk past us with a ton of beach toys and spread out close to the water. The boys take off their shoes and walk slowly toward the ocean and start screaming as they turn and run away from the small waves. The mom takes pictures of them with her phone while the dad runs with the boys, also screaming.

Or maybe the dad is a friend. And the boys aren't brothers. Maybe one belongs to each parent. Maybe they're both named Isaiah.

I ask the other Naomi, "Did you ever make a list about names? And what we should do about that? Because, I mean, look at us. It's like impossible to tell us apart, right?" Yeah, it's a joke I already made, but she seemed to like it.

"Impossible," she says with a small smile. "But no, I just write a lot of lists. And yeah, I also wrote about that DuoTek contest, mostly a bunch of different ideas I thought might be fun to work on."

"I guess I wasn't really listening," I say. I take a bite of the frosting and, oh, oh, is it good! "We all have to do it?"

"Yeah," Naomi says, like it's obvious.

Brianna throws her sandy shovel on the blanket. "I'm going to make people instead!" She stands and runs toward the water and starts to make stick people in the sand, using her foot. The boys near the ocean stop what they're doing and stare at her. She looks like she could take over the whole beach if she wanted to.

"Is there anything you like to be called?" I ask, thinking about how Annie calls me Gnomes. Or Nomes. But I wouldn't want anyone other than Annie to call me that—it wouldn't even make sense. "I mean, any nicknames?"

"Nope," she says, licking her fingers.

"You do too," Brianna says, running toward the blanket, sand flying. I had no idea she was listening. "I call you Queen of All the Queens sometimes because you're so bossy. You could of lived in those castles if I built them, Queen of All the Queens."

The other Naomi looks mad. And embarrassed. Like she wants to pinch her sister's arm. Really hard.

It has to be hard, being Brianna's sister. I want to help.

"So about that project. Do you want to maybe do it together?"

CHAPTER
FIFTEEN

Naomi Marie

"I had an idea for a world explorer adventure game," I say. "We can have cats give the clues."

"I don't know how that would work with my fashion dash idea," she says. "And we did cats already."

"You never told me your fashion dash idea," I say.

"That's because it's in my head."

And that's how it's been going all morning. We are not Girls Gaming the System; we are Girls Who Will Never Finish Making Their Game Because We Can't Agree on Anything. Even those girls who sit in the back and look at videos that show you how to put designs on your fake nails are probably further ahead than us. I tell my so-called partner that, after Julie comes to our table and says those kind of fake-encouraging things adults say when they think you're hopeless.

"We're kind of running out of time," I say. "We only have two classes left until Presentation Day, and that's the deadline, remember?" I usually hand in my school projects early.

"It's not only about the showcase, you know," says NAOMI EDITH. I would call her that out loud if I was feeling mean. But I just want to get our work done. I don't like not getting our work done. I want Julie to tell everyone that we could probably teach the workshop if we wanted to, and then we'd smile and kind of look down because we're being humble.

Yesterday at school I lost the Geo Challenge to Jenn Harlow, who just came back from missing a week of school for a family vacation in Jamaica. When she came back, she walked right up to me with her new blond cornrows and told me her father said that Jamaica would be nothing without tourists. I was so mad! *That's* why I lost the Geo Challenge. Not because I don't know where Rose Hall Plantation is. We go by it every time we visit Aunt Alga, and we say a prayer of remembrance for all the enslaved Africans who were forced to work there. Jenn's family goes to lunch there once, and all of a sudden she's Miss Jamaica.

And now here I am with this *contrarian* (ooh, good word!), who shoots down every suggestion I make but doesn't have any of her own. And the game that was going to be a cool library scavenger hunt/talent contest/pinball/maze is one big mess. It's not even going to be as good as Pong, this "classic" game my dad tried to show me from the olden days that looks like something a doctor would use to hypnotize you so she could sneak a shot or something.

"I know that," I say, "even though you were the one who suggested we work together, remember?" At first it seemed like this was going to work. She was a little bit nice at the beach; plus, I found out she wanted to go to the boardwalk too. And this coding thing is almost okay. It's neutral ground, so we don't have to pretend to like each other's favorite everything. She tells pretty good jokes, sometimes. Before we left the beach we made a list of ideas, and when I slept over at Xiomara's, I didn't even mind her bugging me about wanting to meet "the Other Naomi," which, to be honest, is starting to sound weird to my ears. I even actually thought about bringing her to the library to show Ms. Starr and those bighead Teen Gamez kids what we've been doing, like, BAM. But *now* all I can picture is HER saying a big fat NO to all my ideas, and then Xiomara trying to make us hug it out, or worse, *sing* it out.

"I'm not saying this to be mean, but . . . you're kind of grouchy today," I say as we pack up and go outside to wait for Momma and Tom, who I suspect are late on purpose to give us extra "bonding" time.

"Whenever people say they're not saying something to be something, they really mean to be . . . something," she says, not looking at me.

I don't like people not looking at me. I'm right here.

". . . yeah, that's *usually* true," I say, turning to face her full on, "especially when it's a frenemy like Orchid Richardson.

But not this time, okay?"

She looks up. "How bad is Orchid Richardson?"

"Worse than the worst in every way."

"My mom taught me this thing, this way to help deal with people . . . who are maybe hard to deal with, how you can study them, to figure out what costume they would wear. But it's a really good way to help get through time with people you don't really want to be with."

I hope she's not putting me in that category. I wonder if she talked to her mom about me. I remember the expression on her face when Tom was walking Brianna down to the ocean. I wonder if I looked the same way, because I was thinking Dad should be the only father holding Brianna's hand.

"Your mom?" I'm not sure where to go next. Her face closes up, and she looks away again.

"I mean . . . is there something wrong?" It's like when I think I've found the right puzzle piece, and I keep trying to make it fit because it's so close. "Are you mad about coming over to our house?" I ask. "Because it wasn't exactly my idea, you know." I stop myself. "Not that you're not welcome, though, I mean . . ." I stop. There is nothing I can say to make this string of words get any better.

She shrugs, and now I realize why Momma hates it when I do that.

Fine.

Great. This is going to be great.

★ ★ ★

Momma gives us a plate of the chocolate-butterscotch cookies that we made last night. Now I'm not so sure I want to waste them on NAOMI EDITH THE GROUCH, but if I don't, I won't get any either. She eats three of them really fast, without speaking. *And* she gets up from the table without asking to be excused. And Momma doesn't even say anything, because she's too busy saying everything to Tom. I'm almost too mad to eat, but luckily, I come to my senses and sneak another cookie as Bri leads her to our bedroom. I follow, slowly.

"What should we play-ay?" sings Bri. She doesn't give us a chance to answer. "Family! They're going to the bathroom," she adds, totally unnecessarily, and runs out of the room.

NAOMI EDITH shrugs, looking around the room at my posters of the Williams sisters and Malala, the Muppets collection that I inherited from Dad, the gold cape Momma made me last Halloween, and the tower of board games. I can't tell what she thinks.

Bri comes back, carrying an armful of dolls. "They were taking a nap," she says, which in Briannese means that she was playing with them in the bathroom when Momma said it was time to leave, so she threw them in the laundry basket. Blech. She looks at NAOMI EDITH, who is sitting on my bed (without asking permission). "Did you bring any dolls?"

"Um, no," she answers. I guess she's talking now. "I don't really . . . play with dolls anymore."

"Neither do I," I say quickly. I laser-eye Bri as she opens her mouth, then closes it. "But it's something that I do, you know, as a big sister." Bri is looking at me like she doesn't know who I am, so I grab the Rahel doll quickly and start fluffing her hair.

"Well, we only have Brown dolls," says Bri, looking worried, "so I don't know if you can play with them."

Naomi Edith makes a face. "What do you mean? I'm not allowed to play with your dolls because they're Brown?" Now she looks more than grouchy.

"We only have Brown dolls in this house," says Bri in her talking-like-Momma voice, "because they are a re-fek-shun of our beauty." The other Naomi looks at her.

I speak up. "Everybody's allowed to play," I say. "Bri means that . . . if you don't want to play with Brown dolls, you'll have a problem." I hug Bri's shoulders. "And it's *re-FLEC-tion*," I whisper, but in a kind, big sisterly way. I keep hugging Bri close. I'm like Delphine in *One Crazy Summer*.

"What kind of dolls do *you* have?" Bri asks.

"Like I said, I don't play with mine anymore." Then she goes quiet for a minute, like she's thinking about something she never thought about before. "But I guess . . . you'll need to bring yours when you come to my house." She points to Livia, whose soccer uniform is a little ripped. "Can I have her?"

"*Have* have or play-with have?" asks Bri, putting her hands on her hips like she thinks she's me.

"*Play-with* have, silly," we both answer. Then we look at each other and roll our eyes. Kids.

★ ★ ★

Bri's version of family is basically Bri telling these really long stories and saying stuff like, "Okay, now you put her HERE, and then YOU put HER here," so as long as you move the dolls around the way she wants, it's pretty easy to have a totally different conversation at the same time.

"Those cookies were good," says Naomi Edith after a while. "Did you get them from that bakery you like?"

"We made them last night," I answer. "But Shelly Ann taught me how." I look up and add, "Thanks." I'm pretty sure that was an apology for being grouchy, because I do the same thing sometimes.

"Do you . . . like to cook?" I ask. Momma was all "Get to know her! You might have more things in common!" so I'm trying, but I bet it's more of the *you-play-chess-she-plays-checkers-look-you're-BFFs!* kind of thing.

"Kind of. My dad and I aren't so great about meals," she says. "My mom makes the best French toast! She used to—" She stops. Bri decides that all the dolls are now going to live in a longhouse, mostly because she wants to touch my Lenape diorama. I tell her she can, but that if she's not careful, I get to keep Rahel forever.

"Um, so about your mom . . ." I'm not sure I should bring this up again, but I'm not sure I shouldn't either. "I mean, like, do you talk to her a lot?"

"Yeah, on Skype," she answers. "I'm going to visit her soon."

"Oh, that's good," I say, even though I know that "soon" doesn't mean she can just walk down the street and hang out at her mom's house any time she wants. And I can tell she knows that too—really, really well. She's looking around the room again.

"So do you have any posters of . . . Edith Head?" I ask.

She smiles. "Even better. I have these sketches she made of dresses she designed for Audrey Hepburn. Well, they're really my mom's, but they're still in our house."

I've heard of Audrey Hepburn. My nana said she was almost as glamorous as Lena Horne.

"But even people who weren't, like, obvious movie stars—Edith Head could create the perfect costume, and they'd be all glamorous just from putting on a dress."

"She kind of took her name and made it cool," I say.

"Are you saying Edith isn't a cool name?" she asks, and even though I can tell she's half joking, I don't want to get on the other half's side.

"My friend Xiomara wanted to come over." I change the subject.

"Is she nice?"

"Um, well, she's my *friend*, so she would have to be. . . ." I raise my eyebrows. "Unless you think *I'm* not nice."

She kind of shrugs again, but this time I can tell it's totally joking, and we both laugh.

"We can do a World Explorer Challenge," she says, and it takes me a minute to remember that she's talking about our game. "With cats."

"Or dogs," I answer. "Poodles who like fashion." I start

giggling. "*Poodle* is such a funny name!"

"How about wombats?"

"Aardvarks!"

We spend a few minutes throwing out weird animal names until Bri yells at us for not paying attention to the fact that now the dolls are Arctic explorers. My Venus and Serena dolls are sharing a pair of baby doll socks.

"Maybe one Saturday we can go to Morningstar and my friend Annie can meet us there," Naomi Edith says. "And Xiomara too."

"Maybe," I say as Bri comes over carrying Clue, which she is terrible at playing.

"And Orchid Richardson," she adds.

"That's not even funny," I say, until I realize she's joking. "Very funny."

She grins and shrugs, this time like *Who, me?*

"One game," I say to Bri, "and then let's play something different. Something that none of us has ever played before."

By the time Momma calls us back into the living room, we've played three rounds of Be Friends, which is a game that Auntie Helen gave me last Christmas but I never played because it's one of those cooperative games that my neighbor Feather plays at Urban Wholechild School, and those are always boring. The Other Naomi and I made it into a trivia challenge game, and Bri was happy as long as she got to ring the little bell that was in the box.

Momma and Tom are all smiley at the door, and I feel a little shy all of a sudden; but I smile when I say bye, and I don't stop Bri from giving the Other Naomi a hug.

"Ciao for now, Brianna and Naomi Marie!" Tom says, and he waves.

Excuse you?

"That was nice, wasn't it?" says Momma, in a telling-not-really-asking voice. "Let's relax for a little while, huh? Just the three of us."

I'm quiet as Bri lines up my wizard chess pieces for entry to a dollhouse party. Momma stretches out on the couch.

"It's not everyone who can say she loves bringing her work home," she says, picking up a book. "You'll love this one—I'll let you read it before I take it to school." She pats the seat next to her. "Want to join me? Did you finish reading *The Jumbies* already? Was it scary?"

"Momma, Tom called me Naomi Marie," I say.

"He did?" she says, not looking at me.

"Yes," I say. "He did." And the way I say it makes her put the book down.

"Did it bother you?" she asks slowly. "He's heard me saying it, and I guess it's also the way we were hoping to, uh, resolve the whole, um, name situation."

I can feel a pout coming on, which is so babyish, but it's better than— Never mind. I'm crying.

"Oh, honey!" Momma pulls me into her arms and waits for

me to get to the sniffle stage. "Do you really think I call you Naomi Marie only when I'm angry? I'm pretty sure I say it when I'm glad too."

"Mostly angry," I say. "Sometimes it's Naomi Marie Bennett, sometimes Naomi Marie What Were You Thinking too."

Momma smiles. "I certainly don't mean for it to feel that way. I love saying Naomi Marie. It makes me think of Marie and all the good memories we shared with her." Marie was Momma's best friend from childhood and my godmother who was like a living birthday present and one-woman party up until I was seven. Then she got sick, and sicker, and then she was gone.

"I know! I mean, I'm glad it's my middle name; but sometimes it seems like you're not, or something," I say slowly. "I used to wonder if it made you sad."

Momma doesn't say anything, and we sit for a while.

"I wonder too," she finally says. "I can't tell you all the things that go through my mind—I don't even know them all myself—but I know this: You are growing up into your beautiful wonderful self, *Naomi Marie*"—she puts a finger to my lips—"and I'm so proud of you, and Marie would be so proud of you too. I'm grateful for the time we had on this earth with her, and I would rather have had that, even with the sad parts, than nothing at all. We got to love her, and she loved us, and sometimes loving is hard; but that doesn't make it bad, right?" There are tears in Momma's eyes, but she's smiling at me too. She takes a deep breath. "So from this day forth I declare officially that your name, Naomi Marie, is a celebration of the *fullness of love* that surrounds you, okay?"

Fullness of love . . . I sit and let those words wrap around me. Then Momma tickles me.

I giggle as I squirm away. "But it's also a way to tell me from the Other Naomi."

Momma nods. "Yep. Because it's not like we can tell you apart otherwise, right?"

She smiles and so do I, and I almost tell her that the Other . . . that Naomi (Edith) made the same joke, but I don't. I get *The Jumbies* and snuggle with Momma until Brianna comes over with *Tea Cakes for Tosh*, and Momma and I take turns reading it aloud. And then we have some caramel cake from Shelly Ann's and snuggle some more. I'm glad we still have cake and couch time. And each other.

CHAPTER SIXTEEN

Naomi E.

"What time did you say Annie's dad was picking her up?" Dad calls from the kitchen, where he's making a crazy amount of plate-clattery noise.

I glance at Annie to see if she heard. Mom always called me into the kitchen to ask that kind of question. She said it was rude to ask when the person you were talking about could hear. That always seemed a little silly, because Annie doesn't care at all about politeness, but right now I'm thinking she was right.

But Annie doesn't even look up. She's busy glue gunning some weird piece of material my mom left here onto her backpack. "At four," she says.

"Four," I yell into the kitchen.

"I may need some help before then," Dad yells.

"What kind?" I ask.

"Dinner," he says. That gets Annie's attention. Because I don't think my dad has ever before thought about a meal so many hours before the actual meal. She unplugs the glue gun and without a word walks into the kitchen with me.

Whoa. Dad would kill me if I made a mess like this.

There are grocery bags with stuff spilling out of them hanging off drawers. Pots and pan covers and a colander are piled high in the sink and spread out all over the counter. A knocked-over jar of tomato sauce is leaking onto the floor a little. Each drop, drop, drop makes a new red spot on the gray floor.

"What are you doing?" I ask.

"How can we help?" Annie asks.

"Maybe find the plates that all match each other?" he says, pointing to a cabinet in the dining room that we probably haven't opened since Mom left.

Why is he thinking about finding plates we never use? When there's a whole big mess in the kitchen. "What's going on?" I ask.

"Dinner," Dad says, impatient. "Grandma and Grandpa and Valerie and the girls."

"What?! Today? All of them?????"

Dad pulls a bag of green stuff out of the refrigerator, stares at it for a few seconds, and then puts it on the counter. He looks confused. But then a little annoyed too. With me. "How many times did I tell you?"

It's all . . . Oh, right. "You told me about Grandma and

Grandpa coming Sunday. And then something about Valerie. But you never said it together. I didn't know they were all coming at once. Why couldn't Valerie and Naomi and Brianna come one day and Grandma and Grandpa another? Mom always says about birthday parties that every guest should know at least one other guest. Grandma and Grandpa don't know Valerie!"

"I thought it was time to change that," Dad says.

"Your grandmother knows your grandfather," Annie says. "And he knows her."

Gee, thanks, Annie.

I go into the dining room and look for the plates. If I'd known the other Naomi was coming over, I'd have thought about our DuoTek project. Shoot. She's really, really into it. Like it's super-important to her that our project be one of the best. No. It has to be the absolute best. Even though it's only a class at the Y.

Still. I should have thought about it more, since it has to be done soon. I haven't put anything in the Dump. And I think there's a message I didn't answer. It's just . . . that class. Whenever I think about it, I start getting mad at Dad all over again for the way he signed me up, how it was a sneaky way for me and the other Naomi to be forced together while he spends time with Valerie and Brianna. It's extra-complicated because he seems so happy when we're with them, and I hated it when he was sad all the time.

The plates are in the last place I look: the bottom on the right, behind some big bottles. They're dusty, so I get some paper towels to wipe them off.

It looks like Annie has been doing a full inspection of the ingredients all over the counters and the kitchen table. She knows what Dad can cook, and grilled cheese is by far the most complicated thing he's ever made. "Are you making *lasagna*?" she asks. She looks at my dad as though she hasn't seen him in a while, and he maybe grew a beard and changed his hair color or something. Like she only almost recognizes him.

"Lasagna. Yes. And three-greens salad. And bread."

"You're BAKING a BREAD?" Annie asks, because Annie gets it.

Apparently, so does Dad. "No. Morningstar baked the bread. I'll be *serving* the bread. But I *am* making a lasagna."

"I found the plates," I say. "But why are we being so . . . We never eat off these plates when Grandma and Grandpa come."

"Maybe you could set the table. Well, first clear it off."

He couldn't have thought of this two weeks ago? It's covered—stuff from my cycle-of-nature report and some art projects I did in school that I'm going to mail to Mom and all Dad's newspapers and bills. I find a box in the room that used to be Mom's office, which is still not even close to being a library/TV/music/relax-and-also-we'll-be-allowed-to-eat-in-there room, and I throw all the stuff on the table into the box and push it with my foot into the so-called library/TV/etc. room.

When I get back in the kitchen, Annie is explaining to Dad that you need to cook the meat before you put it in the lasagna. I hope she got to all the important parts, because when a horn honks, Annie grabs her stuff and runs out the door.

"What kind of salad are you making?" Salad! I really wanted to ask that the way Mom and I would, saying the opposite of what I mean. "I know you're a chef-expert at salad making. So how did you decide on this very kind you'll be serving this evening?" But Dad seems to have even less of a sense of humor right now than he usually does.

"Three-greens salad," he says, like that explains everything. I picture three different shades of green crayons. Yum.

I wish Mom could see this. Sort of.

"Dad! Did you and Mom talk about when I could visit, because remember she said that maybe I could go out there and she said that you and she would—"

"Naomi!"

Why is he yelling?

"Look around," he says, annoyed. "You can see this is not the best time to ask. I'm working very hard to make a nice meal, and your mother and I have been playing phone tag, so no. I don't know when. But come on, honey. You can see that now is not the time, can't you?"

I will not cry.

But I must look like I'm about to, because then Dad says, "I'm not mad."

That makes one of us.

I will not cry.

"Did you set the table yet?" he asks.

"I started," I say, and then I walk to the bathroom and close the door.

How come nobody seems to care that I haven't seen my mother in way too long? I can't keep not seeing her. She's my *mom*. I'm doing the best I can. But at the center of everything, in the middle of me, there's nothing. This giant hole of nothing.

I splash cold water on my face. And try to think about something else. But I need to know Dad will remember, so when I leave the bathroom, I write a note to him: *Please talk to Mom about visit.* And I put it in the center of his too-big-for-one-person bed.

Back in the kitchen, I stack up plates. "When are Grandma and Grandpa—"

The door opens before I can even finish, and they're here! Now!

"Naomi, look at you!" Grandma says, her arms stretched for a big hug. Annie says that all her grandparents smell, which is the meanest thing Annie's ever said, but also maybe a little true. I guess Grandma has her own smell too, but I think it's something a little sweet, like vanilla. I wish I smelled like vanilla. Maybe when I'm old.

I hug her and then Grandpa, and before I am even done hugging him, Grandma has the silverware out and is looking for napkins. "I can do it, Grandma," I say.

"And so can I," she says. "Maybe find the napkins and we can do it together."

Dad and I don't ever use napkins. I look under the kitchen sink and in the pantry.

"In the sliding thing," Dad says, pointing. Sure enough, napkins!

Dad keeps looking out the window over the kitchen sink like a kid waiting for the birthday party guests to arrive.

As Grandma and I finish setting the table, I feel this strong wave of . . . feeling, I guess. Of it not seeming fair that now, when all I have here on this side of the country, besides my dad, is my grandparents, I'm supposed to share them with somebody else's family too. I already had to give up my lazy Saturdays with Dad. Now this. What next?

"What time are the other guests arriving?" Grandpa asks. I wonder if he's expecting guests who would make sense. Like maybe Uncle Al. Or Loofie, Dad's best friend from high school, who takes pictures every time he comes over. Not a girl with my name and her baby sister and their mother.

"Valerie and the girls should be here any minute," Dad says.

"So things are getting serious, huh?" I hear Grandpa say in the kitchen.

Huh? Serious? What kind of serious?

"Yeah," Dad says. "Very."

My stomach lurches when Dad *doesn't* say "Serious? No, don't be ridiculous," which is the answer any normal person might expect.

I keep waiting, but he doesn't laugh and say, "I'm kidding!"

And that word, *serious*, especially when combined with *very*, hangs over us the whole time—when they arrive, when they sit at our table—hanging like some sad swinging piñata, ready to burst open.

I doubt I say more than a minute's worth of words the whole time. I'm sure everyone's noticing, but it's almost all I can do to pass dishes from Grandpa to Naomi. Grandma asks about Girls Gaming the System, and I wish I could grunt my answers, because that's all I feel able to do. But I force myself to say, "The teacher's good," and "We've had three classes." When I say "No, we don't have to do a lot of work outside of class," the other Naomi glares at me. I really have to get back to that stupid project. For now I concentrate on cutting the lasagna. With a knife. Because it's really burned.

I can't stop thinking about those two words. *Very serious*, I think as Grandma asks Naomi and Brianna questions about themselves. *Very serious*, when Grandpa fake-laughs as Valerie shares a story that was supposed to be funny but wasn't. *Very serious*, as Dad has that proud look as everyone sits around the table, cutting away the burned parts of the lasagna, talking, fake-laughing.

Very serious.

CHAPTER SEVENTEEN

Naomi Marie

Only two more weeks of Girls Gaming the System, and we didn't get much done today. The Other Naomi was really quiet and mostly sketching things that she didn't show me, even after I said her grandparents were nice (true) and her dad was a great cook (SUCH A LIE). As we're leaving the workshop, I wonder if we'll finish anything in time for Presentation Day. If we don't, we won't even get a chance to enter the contest. All this spending time with her and Tom, and I could end up with nothing to show for it. Just a few weeks ago, I was imagining walking into the library and showing the Teen Gamez Crew what it means to be a CREATOR, NOT A CONSUMER. Now I just want to play some dominoes. With my dad.

"I can't wait to see Dad," I mutter, while Momma and Tom talk about stuff they could have talked about when I didn't have to watch. I think nobody heard, but when Supersonic Momma looks at me with more than a question in her eyes, I wish I could tell her that sometimes I have fun with the Other Naomi, but that doesn't mean this is not completely weird and different and scary and nothing will ever be the same. But I can't say any of that.

"We're sleeping over Daddy's with Xiomara!" Bri says to the Other Naomi.

Momma and Tom stop talking for a minute, but the Other Naomi looks down and says, "That's nice."

Last week we told each other jokes and found out that we both come up with imaginary pranks that we'll never actually do. Today I had a list of things we could talk about while we worked, but she didn't smile once, so I kept it in my pocket. Momma and Tom finally start saying good-bye, and I look down too.

"Bye!" Bri yells over to Tom and the Other Naomi. She shakes her hand free to wave but puts it back in mine right after and squeezes it, like she knows how I feel.

In exchange for a yes to this sleepover, Xiomara's mom said Xiomara had to go to the library, so Momma drops Bri and me off there while she goes on ahead to Dad's with our overnight bags. I wonder if they'll talk for a little while, like they used to, before Tom, or if they'll be shy. And then I want to stop wondering.

Xiomara is standing in front of the library, looking itchy.

"I want to take out some books, but I forgot my card," I say. "Can I use yours?"

Xiomara looks at me and rolls her eyes. "Do you even need a library card? Aren't you on a first-name basis here, like Adedayo?"

"Who's Adedayo?"

"Argh!" Xiomara rummages through her cat purse and pulls out her library card, which she rubs on her jeans before she hands it to me. "You know Adedayo—'No Wifey Here'? 'Souled Out'? The best singer EVER?"

"Okay, yeah, I get it. . . . Thanks for the card. I promise I won't return them late."

I get a bunch of books about game design and programming that Julie mentioned. The Other Naomi doesn't seem like she cares about our project at all anymore; she hasn't added anything to the Dump in ages, and she never even answered my message about the books! Even her grandparents are more into it, and they were obviously born before computers. They asked us some good questions, but she kept changing the subject. I guess Tom had told them that I liked board games, because they brought Find Her!, which I already have, in classic and deluxe versions. But I just said, "Thank you very much," because I am extremely polite.

"After dinner, do you want to see what we do in Girls Gaming the System?" I ask as we walk to Dad's, making sure Bri practices looking left-right-left at every crossing. "The other Naomi and I have a pretty cool game started."

"Sure! Even though I'd really rather meet the Other Naomi in person. When are you going to make that happen? And what do you think of her now? I'm dying to know."

I shrug. "She's okay."

"Like Melissa Banks *weird-but-not-bothering-anyone* okay, or Orchid Richardson *barely-hidden-stank-attitude* okay? There's a difference."

"I know. She's not like either of them. She's . . . okay." I ignore Xiomara's heavy sigh and jump out of the way when Dad opens the door and Bri attacks him with a hug.

"Daddy!" she yells. "We're all here for our SLEEPOVER WITH XIOMARA!!!!"

"What's for dinner?" I ask. I look around, but Momma's already gone.

"Hello to you too," says my dad. "Good to see you, Xiomara." He hugs us both, and I look over his shoulder to the table. Our puzzle is still there, and I feel kind of bad because we haven't made much progress lately.

"I brought wizard chess, but maybe we should focus on the puzzle," I say.

"You just got here. Relax, let's play it by ear," says Dad. "Now, how about a snack?"

"That's what I'm talking about," says Xiomara. "Whatcha got, Uncle Winston?"

It turns out Dad has a pretty nice spread set up for us: sliced apples, super-sharp Cheddar cheese, lemonade, and even chocolate chip cookies!

"Daddy, did you go to Shelly Ann's?" I ask, stuffing a cookie into my mouth. "These are awesome!"

"I made them myself, thank you very much," Dad says, patting his own shoulder. "Next time you come over, maybe instead of a game, we'll do some baking."

I shrug. "Uh, sure!"

Xiomara calls her mom, and when she hangs up, I can tell she got politeness reminders. "Thank you for having me over," she says to Dad.

"You girls are always welcome," Dad says. "Please remember that."

"You don't have to tell me twice," says Xiomara, grinning.

Dad looks like he could use another hug, so I give it to him. He starts showing Bri how to play chess, but before Xiomara and I leave the room, she's changed the game to Wizard Dance Party.

The carpet in my room at my dad's is fluffy and blue; Xiomara and I flop down on top of the giant smiley-face beanbags. "So . . . you never told me—what were the grandparents like? Did they have white hair?"

"Yeah, but they weren't super-old, like I thought they'd be. They were pretty nice, but they asked my mom a lot of questions."

"Did they like you and Brianna?"

"Yeah, I guess. Bri asked them a lot of questions back. And then she invited them to Nana's house in Orlando!"

"Are you guys all going to Orlando together?" Xiomara looks hurt. "I thought I was coming with you this year!"

"Of course we're not going with them; that was just Bri being Bri-ish. They laughed and said they'd love to meet her one day . . . but it was kind of like they were expecting to, like they weren't even surprised when she said that!" I had waited for Momma to say something about it being a family vacation, but she never did. She smiled a lot through that whole lunch: at Tom, at his white-haired parents, even at the Other Naomi, who did *not* always smile back. I counted.

"These cookies are so good," Xiomara says. "I can't believe your dad made them."

"Yeah," I say. "And you know what? *Tom* can't cook at all. I think there was American cheese in his lasagna." So there, Naomi E. for Evil. I go on. "I think it was the first meal he ever cooked. I got ice from the fridge, and there were, like, frozen dinners."

My dad pops his head in. "How are you girls doing? Naomi, what do you think of the beanbags? I thought they were kind of . . . happy."

I groan. "Yes, we're good, Dad, and the beanbags are great. Thank you!" I roll my eyes in the soon-I'll-be-an-annoying-teenager way. Usually he does it back, but he just nods and smiles and closes the door.

"Does my dad seem weird to you?"

"What, the cookies?" Xiomara asks, taking out a small poster of the Milky Way and tacking it to the wall. "That was a pretty awesome snack. Just enjoy the divorced-parents extra-nice guilt glow. It might never go away!" She steps back to look at the poster. "Do you like it? It was in my *Science Stories* magazine, and I know you really need stuff to decorate this place. It's nice that your dad got these beanbags, though. So comfy!"

"Yeah, it's really great—thanks! But um . . . what do you mean?"

"I mean, we haven't had much time to get this room together so that it's really YOU, like your regular room at home. Ooh, speaking of that, have you heard the remix of 'It's So You It's Not Me (At All)'? The best song ever!"

"Adedayo?"

"Of course not. Zuleika. You know, Zuzu. Why are you even talking about Adedayo?"

"ANYWAY," I say, sliding down onto a floor pillow. "I meant, what do you mean about the divorce glow of guilt or whatever?"

"Oh—just that, you know, divorced parents are always trying to make up for being divorced because they want their kids to be happy. I read that on realtalkkids.com after your parents . . . you know."

"But there's nothing to make up for; me and Brianna are okay, Dad lives right in the neighborhood; it's almost like he didn't move out."

Xiomara shrugs. "But he probably still feels guilty. Or maybe he's just worried that Tom is becoming like your dad or something. You know how parents can be kind of sensitive."

"Yeah, that's for sure," I say slowly. Tom is nice to me, but he is NOT IN ANY WAY BECOMING MY DAD, because I already have an awesome dad. I guess I need to show it more.

"Let's work on your computer game," says Xiomara.

"I want to show it to my dad," I say. "Do you mind if I get him?"

"Good idea," says Xiomara. "He probably wants to be all involved and dadly."

"He *is* dadly," I say. "Super-dadly."

"Maybe he'll even get you a new Tech Tock Timekeeper watch!"

"I don't have an old one."

"That's what I'm talking about," she says, nodding.

"You know what?" I say. "Let's play Clue instead. Dad likes that. It's one of his favorites. And we have to keep losing so he can explain to us how to make educated guesses, like a scientist."

"Oh, that sounds fun," says Xiomara, rolling her eyes. I glare at her. "Kidding, kidding. I want Uncle Winston to feel better too."

"Good," I say. "Before I call him, let's make a list of all the ways I can remind him that he'll always be my real dad. My *only* dad."

"But," starts Xiomara.

"What?"

"Nothing," she says quickly. "Well . . . why don't you just tell him you love him and stuff?"

"He *knows* that. I need to do more. I don't want him to look sad, not about me. I want him to know for sure whose side I'm on."

"I don't know if it's about choosing sides. . . ."

"And I have to make sure Tom knows too, right?"

Xiomara throws up her hands. "Yeah, whatever, I've got your back. I still think we can get a Tech Tock Timekeeper watch out of this somehow, though."

I pick up my smiley beanbag and throw it at her.

CHAPTER EIGHTEEN

Naomi E.

I've never been so happy about a rainy day. A soaking, rainy day. Heavy, endless rain that means Annie's after-school soccer practice is canceled, which Annie says happens almost never, so yay! Keep raining, rain! I want to hang out with my always-busy friend!

Mom couldn't Skype with me over the weekend, so we talked and texted when we could. And this morning she sent me a text: **Need to see your face! Can we Skype at 4?**

I guess I needed to see hers on this yucky, gray day too, because, finally! "Mom!"

"I know," she says. "It's been ridiculous."

"What do you mean?" I say. "I enjoy not talking to you for so long. It makes me feel so . . . grown-up." But instead of laughing, we both shrink a little bit in our seats. Saying the opposite of what you really think, turns out, isn't always funny.

"Well, Naomi girl. I haven't only wanted to see your face for the sake of seeing your face, though that's a pretty good reason right there."

"It is," I say.

"Your dad and I have been trying to figure out when you can come out here."

Oh good! I thought all the quiet from Dad on this subject meant he was too busy being serious, very serious, about Valerie to think about schedules and airplanes.

"But it got complicated because somehow I forgot that Dad and I agreed you're too young to fly by yourself all the way across the country and—"

"I am not!" I say, wondering if it's true. I could watch a bunch of movies and eat a ton of snacks. "Or I could bring Annie and not fly alone!"

"Well, I'm afraid that's not your decision to make. It's one made by your father and me." I hear her cell phone ring, and she holds a finger up to the screen, to me, and says, "One sec."

While she talks to whoever she has to talk to, an empty feeling starts swirling through my insides. If I can't fly to California, if I can't see my mother, how am I going to . . . ? How can I keep not seeing my mother? How does anyone think this is okay?

Mom says, "I'll get it to you before five, I promise, but I have to go now," to whoever's on the phone and turns back to me. "Sorry. So I don't know what you're going to think of this, but

I think it's pretty exciting news. Or at least I'm really excited."

I have to act happy when Mom tells me about her next job, because she's doing what she always wanted to do and I'd have to be a horrible and selfish person to be sad about it, even if it means I have to wait longer to see her. I hope the smile on my face looks more brave than fake. Because I'm trying!

"Do you remember Myla? My assistant on *Frog Ballet Love Triangle*?"

"The one who had cats named Sidney and Ketchup?"

"You are an oddball." Mom smiles. "But yes. Well, she's coming out to California at the end of June!"

"And you're really excited about that?" I half say and half ask.

"Yes, because she's going to stay in my apartment!"

"I thought it was really small," I say. When I imagined my visit to California, I saw it as a long relaxing party, both of us in lazy-day clothes, lying around, eating popcorn and takeout, everything within reach.

"It is. And so is her place."

"I remember," I say. It smelled like cat.

"But I don't think that will bother me too much when I live there this summer."

And now I understand why Mom needed to see my face, because I'm pretty sure it looks like I won the Showcase Showdown and the lottery and a free lifetime supply of cupcakes and five puppies at once. I'm like a one-girl party, jumping up and down and only half listening as she explains that she couldn't figure out how to make my visit to California work, since she was going to work on one job and then another right away, but then after she talked to Myla, who talked about wanting to break into TV and movies, she was able to pass her next job along to Myla. Which gets us to the important part: she's taking off all of July so she can have a whole month with me!!!

As we're saying good-bye and I'm saying, "I love you and I'm so happy and this is the best news ever," I hear Annie talking to my dad in the kitchen, so I make Mom wait so Annie can say hello because I think maybe Mom misses Annie too and maybe Annie misses my mom and they have this awkward *hi, hi* conversation and then Mom has to go and I say, "Guess what!" to Annie, who forgot to bring a raincoat or umbrella and looks like she walked through lawn sprinklers. On her hands.

"Um, I get to meet that other Naomi?"

"WHAT?" I ask. "Let's go in my room," I say, so we leave the not-even-close-to-being-a-library/TV/music/relax-and-also-we'll-be-allowed-to-eat-in-there-but-at-least-there-is-a-computer-in-there room.

We flop down on my bed, which is wrinkly and gross because I haven't made it in weeks, and I tell her about my mother's plans for July, and we think about some of the things we can all do together on the days Annie doesn't have soccer camp.

And then I pull out a stack of picture books. "Please?" I say.

She looks through the pile, laughs her sort of crazy laugh, and pulls out one book. She takes a look at the first illustration and then holds it out for me to see, like she's a teacher and I'm . . . kindergarten.

Showing me the cover, she says, "A boy and a nice lion look out a window."

She opens the book. "A squirrel is in a tree. A boy takes his lion to school. A girl brought her bunny. One boy has a backpack on his head, and he's maybe a zombie."

She turns to the next picture and grins. "In the classroom, there are books and weather things. The boy and lion stare at a spider. An alligator might eat a cat."

And then we're both laughing.

"Can I do the next page? I ask. She hands me the book. We could do this all day. We could do this forever.

Before long, Annie's hungry, and we go searching through the pantry until she finds some probably-too-old Girl Scout cookies.

"You go first," I say, offering the box to her. She's a brave eater.

"How's stuff with the other Naomi?" she asks, sniffing at a Thin Mint.

"Where did that come from?" I ask.

"You spend a lot of time with her. I think it would be cool to meet her." She bites into the cookie and her face makes me think we'll be throwing out the whole box, but then she reaches for another.

Dad walks in and says, "Aren't those cookies from last year?"

Annie and I nod. She asks, "Want one?"

Dad takes one.

"Mmm . . . cookies," he says. "Oh! Before I forget, I was on the phone with Valerie, and we were talking about having a celebration after your last club meeting."

"What would we even be celebrating?" I ask.

"Your hard work and open minds? And isn't that the day your projects are due?"

Ugh. That project. I told the other Naomi I would add a list of possible quizzes and I didn't. I shrug. "I guess." Now I feel bad. I have to get back to that stupid project.

"So we can all celebrate that."

Right. Sure. We can celebrate. My hard work.

Annie elbows me. And then elbows me again. And then I get it and ask, "Can Annie come?"

"I think that's a terrific idea," Dad says. "The more the merrier."

I wonder if that's always true.

CHAPTER NINETEEN

Naomi Marie

"Nice pants, Bennett," says Mikey as he runs by. I look down at my leggings. The pattern is just like the black-and-white-marbled composition notebooks we use at school. They ARE nice pants, so I don't know why he thinks that's an insult. Oh yeah, right—this is Mikey we're talking about: he doesn't think.

I ignore him and turn to Xiomara as we leave the classroom. We figured out today that there are only twenty-seven more days of school, and it's Friday, so no Mikey for two days—I want to celebrate! "Hey, do you think our moms will let us go to the playground for a little while?"

Xiomara nods. "My mom will say yes if your mom does, so let's go ask your mom together first. I'll sing for her; she can't resist that!"

"Yeah, you'll win her over with the . . . power of your voice," I say as we walk down the hall to the library.

"Can you start calling me Xio?" says Xiomara, drawing it out in a really dramatic way, like SEEEE-oh. "It sounds like I'm already a star that way."

"Um, okay," I say. "I guess it's a good idea to have a nickname ready just in case you have to spend every Saturday with a girl who has the exact same name as you someday."

"Come on, you have to admit Naomi Marie sounds kind of elegant. And you said she's not that bad," says "Xio." "Are you almost ready to introduce us? I think it would be so cool to hang out together!"

"Well, she was telling me about her friend Annie," I say slowly, lowering my voice as we walk into the library even though school's over. Momma has a rep to protect, so I try to follow the rules even when I don't have to. "Maybe it won't be awkward with all four of us. We can take Shotsie for a walk . . . maybe go to Shelly Ann's."

We walk into Momma's tiny office, and she's not there.

But Tom is.

"You must be Xiomara," Tom says, like he belongs in my school. At Momma's desk.

"Xio, actually," says Xiomara. She lifts up her head like she's fancy. "And you are . . . ?"

"Tom," he says, smiling. He turns to me. "Hi, Naomi Marie. Your mom had to run Bri over to Dr. Johnson's. She got sick and threw up at school. Val asked me to meet you, and here I am." He holds up a white paper bag. "I've even got Shelly Ann's."

"WHAT?!" I drop my backpack, and the water bottle inside makes a big clank. "Is Bri okay?" I ask. "How come nobody told me?"

"Tom's telling you now," says Xio, oh so helpfully.

"It sounds like she'll be fine," says Tom quickly. "Don't be scared."

"I'm not scared," I say, but I know my voice is shaking. "But I can feel any way I want to—it's *my s*ister!" *And you're in my mom's office like you belong, and I just want to cover my ears and scream.*

"I mean . . . your mom just wanted to be careful. There are so many viruses going around right now. She checked in a few minutes ago, and she said you can call her if you want."

"I do want," I say, picking up my backpack and trying to speak past the lump in my throat. "I mean, this is *my* family. And Bri doesn't go to *school*, it's *playgroup*." I know I sound worse than snotty, but it's like there's a different me in control. Momma's gone, and my little sister's sick. . . . Tom's trying to be . . . *dadly*, saying "Bri" and wanting to bribe me with Shelly Ann's. I'm not having it. And he shouldn't know doctor stuff. That's *personal*.

"Sorry. Playgroup," says Tom. "Wherever she was, she puked. Big-time." He smiles. I don't.

I can hear Xio hold back a giggle.

I turn my back on Tom and call Momma.

"Hi, sweetie pie, I'm so sorry to surprise you like this, but I had to pick Bri up from Little Nubians, she threw up during free play, but she's fine, they think it's a twenty-four-hour bug, and

Tom was around—" Momma sounds breathless, and I know I should say, *How's-Bri-I'm-okay,* but . . .

"Why didn't you get Daddy?" I blurt out. "Since this is a *family* matter." I look right at Tom when I say that, and it feels good when he looks down. That other me has taken over.

She sighs. "Well, your father was tied up on a conference call. I had to run . . . and I didn't want to leave you hanging, honey."

"Why was he visiting you?" I ask. "Did he get fired from his job?" I hear Tom snort behind me, so I guess he knows what we're talking about. I move a little farther away. "I mean, I'm just thinking about him and his daughter. He has to spend so much money buying all those frozen dinners since we already know he can't cook."

"Naomi Marie—"

"See!" I say. "You're saying it when you're upset!"

"Ugh, sorry, sorry," she says, and sighs again. "My dear sweet Naomi Marie, I know this was a surprise and maybe not the kind you usually hope for. I didn't want to just text you and have you deal with this all alone. It's a little crazy right now, and I have to pay attention to your sister. It sounds like we'll be home this evening. Tom can tell you everything. You can make it work right now, yeah? I know you can. Tom can take you over to your dad's if you want."

"I just—"

"Thank you, honey. The doctor's back. I love you." She hangs up.

"I love you too, Momma," I say slowly, even though she can't hear me anymore. "And I hope Bri's really all right."

I stand there with my back still turned, but now it's mostly because I need to fix my face before I look at Tom or Xio.

"Everything okay?" asks Tom softly. "I wrote down everything your mom reported after the doctor checked Bri out. Even her 'ums.'"

"Momma hardly ever says 'um,'" I say, looking at him and trying to smile a little. "Everything's okay. But . . . I'd like to see your notes."

He hands them over, and they're in a list, nice and numbered, just the way I like. I wonder if he found that out about me or if it's just a coincidence, but I don't ask. Xio reads over my shoulder.

"Thank you," I say, very softly, but I know he hears. "Um, can you take me to my dad's apartment?" I look at Xio and raise my eyebrows. She gets it right away.

"And me?" she asks quickly. "We can do our homework together."

I smile and mouth, Thank you. I'm not ready to be by myself in Tom's car.

"Sure," says Tom. "As long as you guys can direct me." At least he doesn't know *that*. Then it would be too weird.

"I'll, um, call my mom first," says Xio. "I'll tell her that I can walk home from your dad's place."

While she does, Tom and I stand there, not really looking at each other. I don't feel like that other me anymore, but I don't feel like myself either.

★ ★ ★

Tom's car radio turns on when he starts the engine, and it's loud—I bet he was singing, because he shuts it off real quick, like he's embarrassed, and clears his throat. He glances at me in the rearview mirror, but I look out of the window and pretend I don't feel Xio nudging me. I give him Dad's address, and he puts it in his GPS, which I'm surprised this car has because it looks OLD.

"How old is this car?" I ask. "It doesn't seem safe."

Tom looks at me sideways. "I don't have a car, actually. This one belongs to my neighbor George. I wanted to get to you right away, and he came to the rescue. He calls it the G-DOGmobile, and I have every confidence in it."

I turn away and think eye-rolly thoughts.

"So, Xio," he says. "Has Naomi Marie told you about the coding club? You might be interested in joining the girls for the next session."

"It sounds really cool," says Xio. "I was thinking that I could make a karaoke game or something."

He says "the girls" like we're a pair or something. NOT.

"What do you think, Naomi Marie?" he asks. "Maybe you three can all work together. And Naomi's friend Annie—the four of you could be a team."

"That's exactly what I was thinking!" says Xio, and I glare at her.

Tom clears his throat again. "The girls have a project presentation coming up. Maybe you can join our little celebration afterward." He pauses. "How's the project going, Naomi Marie?

Naomi doesn't say much about it."

Because she doesn't do much about it is what I want to say, but I don't. I won't sell her out like THAT. "It's fine. My dad will help with it too. It's a good thing he's always here for me," I say, a little more loudly than I need to. "I don't know what I'd do without him. He's the best father a girl named Naomi could have."

Xio elbows me hard, but I just blink a few times and stare straight ahead.

"Your father is a great guy," says Tom quietly. "And we have a lot in common."

"How do *you* know?" I ask, not caring how rude I sound. Xio's staring at me with her mouth open.

"We've met," says Tom. "We've talked."

What? Now *my* mouth is open.

"He certainly loves you and your sister very much," Tom adds as he pulls up in front of Dad's place. "And I can see why."

Well, now I know Tom's a total liar, because I'm not that nice to him, especially today. But I don't really know what to do except mumble "Thank you" and follow Xio out of the car. Tom smiles, and waves at my dad when he opens his door and waves me and Xio inside. My dad waves back at Tom. All this waving is making me feel sick.

"I don't feel so good," I say to Xio. "Maybe you should go home now."

Xio looks at me for a minute and then says, "I have to walk Shotsie anyway." She stomps off, and I want to run after her.

But I don't.

CHAPTER TWENTY

Naomi E.

When Mom and I talk or Skype now, it's all about plans—what we'll do when she's here. For a whole month! We're going to drive to Jones Beach. And she's going to take Annie and me to a place with indoor trampolines, and we can stay as long as we want, jumping for hours, because Mom always wanted to have a trampoline for me but our backyard wasn't big enough.

"So how's that class going? You haven't talked about it at all, but I've been wondering. Did you end up liking that girl you told me about?"

That girl. The other Naomi.

"I guess. It's just . . ." And I can't even think of what it just is, but I know it has something to do with the work I haven't done on our DuoTek project. "I don't really like the class," I say. "Or I guess it's okay, but I wish we didn't have to do a project."

And that's not even the whole truth. I feel guilty, very guilty, that I haven't done any work. Tomorrow's the last class before the whole big presentation thing we're having on the last day, and so far, we've made no progress. Naomi Marie wants everything to be so complicated! Like instead of having to go through a maze, she wants it to be a maze within a maze with three puzzles hidden inside and a quiz at the end.

"When's it due?" Mom asks. "You're not going to let it turn into a whole Vasco da Gama thing, right?"

Okay, so maybe I put off my explorers diorama in third grade and maybe we didn't even have a shoe box in the house and it's possible we sent my dad to the store just to *buy shoes* at five o'clock the night before it was due. And there may have been some crying and freaking out involved too. Maybe. But I guess Mom forgot her promise not to bring up my most epic meltdown ever again.

"Do what you need to do. The class is over in two weeks, Naomi. Just get it done."

Dad always leaves me alone when I'm Skyping with Mom, but he walks right in and lowers his head so she can see him. "Hello, Sarah," he says.

"Hi, Tom. Oh, wow. Your hair got long!"

"Did it?" he asks, reaching his hand up to the back of his neck. "Yeah, I guess it did. When you have some time, I'd like to talk to you about some things."

Hello? Mom? Dad? This is my time to talk with Mom. I clear my throat the way Ms. Gomez does when she wants the class to stop talking. They ignore me.

"Well, sure. No problem. I'll see you in July."

"I know," Dad says. "There are a few things I want to discuss before then."

"A man of mystery," Mom says.

"Who probably wants to let his daughter talk to her mom for a little while," I say.

Dad sort of fake-punches my head the way he and his friend Loofie give each other noogies, but then he smiles and waves good-bye to Mom and leaves the room.

Mom sips from the mug next to her, then makes a face. That means her coffee got cold. She pushes the mug away and says, "I wonder what that's about."

I am nearly sure it's about Valerie. I wonder how much Mom knows. If she even knows anything. She's heard me talk about Dad's friend Valerie's daughter. But does she know that *friend* is maybe more than *friend*? "Very serious," even?

"Well, one thing I know for sure. There's no way it's about him and Valerie," I say. "Because he hardly ever wants to talk about her, and he definitely never wanted me to be instant best buddies with her daughter. He finds it totally boring to talk about her."

Mom doesn't say anything, doesn't even laugh, and I think I might have taken some steps in the way-wrong direction.

More silence.

Of course she doesn't want to think about the man who used to be her husband being in a relationship or whatever with some other woman.

"We never really talk about that, do we, Naomi?" she says.

I push the chair away from the desk and see my face grow smaller on the picture-in-picture on the laptop. "No," I say. "We don't. I guess—I don't really know how to talk to you about Dad going on dates or whatever."

Mom presses her lips together and nods. "I understand," she says. "But the answer is, the same way you talk to me about everything. I hope I'll go on to meet someone else at some point, and that's what I want for your father too."

"So you're really okay with Dad and Valerie being . . ." I can't even finish.

"Together," she says. "Yes, I am. You can talk to me about anything. I mean it."

I nod.

"I'm concerned about you, keeping everything inside, to yourself."

"I know," I say. Because the truth is, I'm a little worried about that too.

After we say good-bye, I stay on the computer and open the DuoTek project.

In class last week, we came up with a lot of ideas, but as I play around with our project now, I realize I have no idea how to do all the DuoTek things the other Naomi does so easily. I have to go back into the tutorial to figure some stuff out.

I keep trying to see if I can take what we did—really, what she did—and find a way to get some of my ideas into it so she knows I'm trying, at least. I add some stairs, make sure they work, and save the changes, thinking the other Naomi will be mad she didn't come up with that idea. I'm so excited I figured out how to do it that I'm almost having fun. In fact, I think I really am!

I send her a message in the Dump.

Hey! I added stairs so there are two levels now. I can work on the bottom and you can work on the top if you want. Let's talk about how we want the game to end. We still have lots of time to get it done.

I'm deciding between adding a wave feature or a race when Dad walks in again. "Working on your DuoTek project?" he asks, leaning in to look at the screen.

I usually love doing things with my dad, but not this. Not today. I close the laptop.

"Don't stop," he says. "Were you working on your project? Aren't you and Naomi Marie supposed to work on it together? I could call Val and see if she wants to bring—"

I stand up and walk out of the room. But once I'm out, I can't even think of where I want to be. Not the kitchen. Not my room. Maybe the backyard? No, it's muddy from all the rain. What I want is to not be talking about the other Naomi and Valerie with my dad, because it feels like that's all that really matters to him lately. I march into the hallway and sit under the painting of three girls sitting on a bull. Mom wanted to take it when she moved out, but I asked her not to. It would have left such a sad hole.

"Are you mad about something?" Dad asks, a question in his voice that makes me think he's expecting me to say, *Mad? Me? That's hilarious! I'm the opposite of mad!*

If he were paying attention, there wouldn't be any question at all. He would have noticed my stompy march out of the room. Or how I'm biting my lip and clenching my teeth so tight, some molars might break. And sitting under a painting of a bull in the hallway.

I'm almost sure I don't have the right words for this, but really, I wish he could just know. That he didn't need me to explain. Why can't he get it, like Mom would?

"I am mad," I say, a little surprised that my voice sounds way more sad than mad.

"Really? What's up?"

I should have talked this through with Mom. She's so good at helping me get out of this stupid stuttery place I get stuck in when I'm mad.

Dad stands against the hall opposite me and slides down so he's sitting too. I've lived here since I was born, and I don't think anyone has ever sat in this hallway before.

I wait for Dad to ask questions, the way Mom would, but he's waiting too. Maybe he has no idea what else to do. I look down and see my thumbs are tucked into my fists, the way Mom's always were when she was fighting with Dad.

I dig my heels into the old rug and move them back and forth, like I'm digging a little hole.

I need to start talking.

So I do.

"When you signed me up for that class, without asking me, I really hated that. It felt like you were trying to trick me into being friends with the other Naomi."

He opens his eyes wide but otherwise looks the same, nodding his head. He still doesn't say anything.

I cross my legs and take a deep breath, getting ready to say more, but then Dad asks, "Don't you like the club?"

"It's okay," I say. "There are a lot of things I'd rather do than learn DuoTek, though. Which is why it felt so bad that you signed me up without even asking me. And it's more a class than any kind of club."

He nods again. "Sweetie, can we go in the kitchen? Or the living room? My back is killing me. Hallways are not meant for sitting."

I stand and then reach for his hands to help pull him up. He follows me into the living room. I flop in the big chair, and he sits on the edge of the shabby blue couch, which is actually starting to look more like a shabby gray couch. He leans toward me. "I did want you to have a chance to spend time with Naomi. I know you two will really hit it off. You're both such good kids and have so much in common, and Val and I—"

There's an old video of me when I was three. I have my

hands on my dad's cheeks and my nose is touching his and I keep saying, "Listen to me. Listen to me." I really want to do that now. Instead I say, "That's not really true, Dad, that we have so much in common. Or maybe it is, but you didn't even let us find out, really. You made us hang out all the time, and she might like DuoTek but it's really not something I . . . I don't know."

"Okay. But now that you've had time with Naomi Marie, what do you think?"

It's like it always is. Dad's practically wearing a sign that says Tell Me You Like Her. I Need You to Like Her.

"She's okay. No, yeah, I like her. But do you know what I'm saying, Dad? About signing me up? And everything."

Dad sighs. "I know I'm not a perfect parent," he says. "I feel like I'm doing the best I can, but I'm going to try harder. I have to try a little harder." He's quiet, and then he stands and says, "We haven't eaten today. Come with me."

I follow him into the kitchen, and he opens the refrigerator. I checked this morning, and I'm almost sure there's nothing in there. I hope I'm wrong; I'm getting hungry! He reaches in, and when he pulls out an old multicolored pineapple, I start laughing.

He walks over to the trash, and it makes a thud when it hits the bottom. "But wait. What about that zoo camp? You liked that zoo camp."

"I wanted to do zoo camp. But then I didn't like it. Remember where the monkeys slept? And how they kept talking about how we'd get to see where the monkeys sleep?"

"Oh," he says. "They slept in a room. Right."

"But this isn't only about the class. Or maybe it is," I say.

"The club—class, I mean—is over soon. And I won't do that again, sign you up for anything without discussing it with you. Deal?" He sounds like he really is trying harder.

"Deal."

I'm glad about that, but I also want more than that. I want him to understand what I want without needing to explain it all the time. And I want him to tell me that he still likes doing things with me. Just me.

CHAPTER TWENTY-ONE

Naomi Marie

"How's Bri?" I ask Dad as he hugs me tight. A tiny, guilty part of me is relieved that he's probably so worried that he won't even notice that Xio left.

"What happened to Xiomara?" Dad asks.

So much for that.

"I think I'm getting sick, so I told her she'd better go," I answer. "Have you gotten any news?"

"Everything's fine. Sorry, I thought Tom already told you. Your mom and Brianna are on their way home. Your sister will probably be kind of grouchy for a day or two." He puts an arm around my shoulders as we go inside. "*You* know how that is. When you're not feeling well and all."

We're both quiet as we sit at his kitchen counter for a snack.

"It was nice of Tom to drop you off," says Dad. "He's a good guy."

I don't say anything.

"We've had a chance to talk, you know," continues Dad. "He's a good guy."

"You just said that," I mumble.

"Sorry . . . ," says Dad. "I'm glad that . . . it's working out."

"You're glad?" I ask, looking up at him. "Really glad?"

"It's . . . complicated, Naomi Marie," says Dad. "But yes. I am."

"I guess you heard," I say. "About my name."

"I did. Pretty funny, huh?"

"I'm not laughing," I say.

"How are you feeling about it?" he asks.

I shrug. "It's elegant, I guess." I finish my crackers and cheese and look in the fridge for some apple slices.

"You never have enough food," I blurt out. *Wait—I don't want to be mean to my dad too too.* I don't know what's wrong with me.

He doesn't seem to notice. "You're right. I need to think about how quickly you're growing," he says. He raises his right hand. "From now on, I pledge to be well stocked at all times."

"Think chips," I say. "And maybe caramel corn. You can always have pizza dough and mozzarella on hand too."

"Let's make a shopping list for me and then a list of what we're going to do next," says Dad. "I can take you home now, or, if you want, you can stay here and do your homework. And then maybe we'll have time for a quick game of Mad Gab."

"This is my home too," I say, taking a sip of ginger tea. I bet Tom doesn't even have ginger tea in his house.

"It makes me happy to hear you say that," says Dad, grinning. "Because it's the truth. You'll always have a home with me, because you will always have my heart."

There's a lump in my throat so big I can't even swallow my tea, so I just nod.

"And," he continues, "I'll always be your dad. Nothing will change that." He pauses. "Whatever happens, nobody wants to change that."

"Are you sure?" I ask. I take a deep breath. "Because Tom . . ." I don't even know what I want to say.

"Tom's cool, and he cares about your mom and you girls very much," says Dad slowly, like he's been practicing. "And he knows how much I do, and respects that."

"So nothing's going to change?"

He smiles. "Circumstances always change," he says. "But I'll say it a million times if you need me to: I'll always be your dad." He hugs me tight.

I want to just enjoy the hug, but I pull back for a second. "So . . . if Momma and Tom keep . . . dating . . . will he be more like . . . Uncle Kevin?" Uncle Kevin is my dad's friend from college. They sing silly songs when they get together, and Uncle Kevin tells us embarrassing stories about "back in the day." Sometimes he brings pictures—there's one where Dad had a frohawk and Uncle

Kevin had his hair in cornrows! Now they're both bald.

"Sort of," says Dad. Then he chuckles. "But, heh, we probably can't call him 'Uncle Tom.'" He starts full-on laughing, and after a minute so do I. My dad's got jokes.

"Anyway, Tom and I can coexist," Dad says. "We've each got our own shine."

I'm not sure what Tom's shine is. Choosing food that other people make? I guess I can give it time.

"Give it time," Dad says. OH MY GOODNESS, DAD'S MAGIC TOO. "We got this. We can each shine our own light without dimming anyone else's."

"What does that mean?"

"Well, like, you can be fully you without . . . *diminishing* Bri, right? And vice versa?"

I nod. Even when Bri makes me mad, I don't want to make her *less*.

"Sometimes there's more room in our lives than we realize. We can grow and grow, and the world around us can too. So . . . maybe *Naomi Marie* is on her way to being a *fuller* Naomi. Maybe Naomi Marie will shine even more, and her light will help others do the same."

He's getting a little speechy, but I kind of get it, I think. Maybe I don't mind not being who I used to be. "I'll give it time," I say. "And I'll shine."

"That's my girl. Ready to play Mad Gab? Or should we finally finish this puzzle?"

"I should call Xiomara—I mean Xio—first." I was rude. Even though I know she's got my back no matter what, I want to say out loud that I'm sorry. I'll probably have to watch the Off-the-Street audition round of *Vocalympians!* in return, but Xio's worth it.

"Go ahead. I'll set up. Puzzle or Mad Gab? Or do you have a better idea?"

I do, actually. I want to show him the game *I'm* making. I want to show him that he is my one and only dad, forever and ever, the only dadly person in my life. And even if the Other Naomi doesn't care about the presentation and contest, I do. I started a whole new DuoTek project, all my own. I stopped checking the Dump a while ago; she never does anything, and she never answered my questions, so why bother? She can sit there and have quietude while I do the presentation if she wants. This is my own fresh start. I worked hard, and I'm kind of excited—I think it's good! It's an adventure game, and my character looks a little like Bri. She has to use different skills to get through different worlds. I'll put the Other Naomi's name on it anyway, just to be nice. And I left some open code so she can add that fashion idea—it was cool, kind of like paper doll spies.

"Can I show you what I've done with DuoTek?" I say to Dad.

"Your Saturday thing?" he says. "I'd love to see it. Did you figure out how to program the surfboard over the waterfall?"

"Yep," I say, smiling. "The player had to name three Coretta Scott King Book Award winners and a Newbery to make it over safely."

"You are your momma's girl," he says, smiling and ruffling my hair.

"Yours too," I say quickly. "We're game buddies forever, remember?"

"And ever," he replies. I get up so he can sit at the computer. "So, am I your first player?" he asks. "I'm honored."

"The honor is all mine," I say very grandly, and we both laugh. "It's not totally finished yet, though. But you can play up to level six. I taught myself some code that we didn't get to in the workshop." I don't add that Naomi E(vil) never really did anything in class and just sat there the whole time while I entered code last Saturday. Whenever Julie came around, we both pretended everything was cool, but it wasn't.

But my game is, I think. I really, really do. It almost doesn't matter about her not helping, because I had fun, and I'm proud of myself. I've got to figure out a way to make sure the Teen Gamez Crew sees this.

She could have messaged me back, though.

"Come on, let's do this," he says, rubbing his hands together. I show him how to move the pixies, and he's on his way.

"I'm proud of you, honey," he says, after a few minutes of playing. "Proud, but not surprised."

I try to put everything I'm not sure how to say into two words. "Thanks, Dad."

He gets to the glitchy part where the Bri-pixie is supposed to juggle apples, but I haven't figured out how to program it so she can pick them up from the ground.

"I'm a little stuck there," I say. "But I'll figure it out soon."

"I know you will," he says. "Be sure to show me the whole thing as soon as you're done."

After a pause, I say, "There's a presentation. Do you want to come? But I don't know . . ." I don't know if the Other Naomi is going to like my game, and I don't know if my dad and Tom can both be there for the presentation, and I don't know how to program my life so that there aren't any glitches.

"Let's talk about it with your mother," he says, like he knows what I'm thinking. I should write a book about magic parents. But maybe kids wouldn't want to read that. Too scary. "Either way, we'll have a showing right here, okay? Show your uncle Kevin. . . . Your aunt Ramona and her kids are coming to visit in a couple of weeks. You know they'll all want to see it. No rules against two presentations."

"We can make two presentations the new rule," I say.

"Okay," he says. "Show me what you're trying to do here. Maybe I can help. You know I won't do your work for you—"

"—but you'll create opportunities for my work to shine," I finish, smiling. "Momma still says that too."

"We're always a team in that respect," he says as he stands so that I can sit again. "You'll never have to choose. Your mom and I are both here to help you shine."

CHAPTER TWENTY-TWO

Naomi E.

I wish I could get credit for the things I *think* about doing. Because up in my brain, I'm a really nice person. Super-nice. Someone who always thinks she can do the right thing.

Like whenever I finally get my room all cleaned up, I truly believe—I really do!—that I'll be able to keep it that way forever. But after just a couple of days, there's always a pile of papers on the desk and books all over the floor and five cups I didn't take back to the kitchen and dirty clothes that never made it into the hamper.

Because as Dad and I walk to the Y, I remember that all week I kept checking to see if the other Naomi got back to me about the upstairs/downstairs idea, but she never did. And she didn't do any work on our project at all. Nothing. So I didn't either. She was the one who was all into it. I had thought we'd get it done, she'd be happy, and I'd at least be finished with that class knowing I finally chipped in and helped. But the other Naomi gave up. So I guess we'll have to hang our heads in shame when Julie asks if anyone wasn't able to get their project done in time.

"Don't forget, we're going out with Valerie and the girls after class," Dad says. We're walking fast because we always leave home later than we should.

"And Annie and Xio," I say.

"That's right! Annie will get to meet Valerie and Naomi Marie and Brianna!"

"Yeah," I say.

Luckily, we make the endless light at Scary Boulevard so I'm not super-late. Just regular-late.

I'm dreading class, but at least it all ends today. Dad and I can go back to our lazy Saturday mornings! Just the two of us. I say good-bye and walk down the make-me-choke-from-chlorine-smell halls to the classroom, and as usual, I'm the last one there.

The other Naomi is wearing this really cool turquoise shirt, and as I sit down next to her, I say, "That shirt looks so good on you!" And she gives me a big smile. And I think, *Hey! Everything is really going to be all right!*

Julie steps to the front of the room, and everyone goes quiet.

"I'm going to give you a few minutes right now to run through your projects, make sure everything's working, and then we'll move forward with presentations."

A knot tightens in my stomach. "We should tell her," I say to the other Naomi. "Before everyone starts showing what they did. Let's get it over with." When I was little, I used to like to pull a Band-Aid off slowly (underwater, when possible), but now I believe in getting hard things over with quickly.

The other Naomi is scratching at a tiny piece of something on the keyboard when she asks, "Tell her what?"

What does she think??? "That we weren't able to finish," I loud-whisper. "That we don't have anything to show!"

Why won't she look at me?

She says something really quiet, not at all to me, under her breath. Is she scared? "Come on, Naomi," I say. "Let's tell her. . . ."

"But we did finish," she says, louder now. "Or I guess I should say, *I* finished. Since you—" And then she's back to talking under her breath.

The two girls sitting in front of us turn around and give us this long stare, a silent way of saying "BE QUIET!!!" But the other Naomi is being plenty quiet now.

"What do you mean?"

She opens a project and starts playing around with it. I ask, "Hey, where are the stairs I put in?" And then I realize that it's not even our project at all. It's something completely new. Something I had nothing to do with.

"I made a new game since you didn't seem interested in it.

I thought it was fun, so I did it, and it came out great, no thanks to you."

I feel stung. And it doesn't make sense, because she's right. I mostly didn't want to do it. But I also finally did the right thing, and she completely ignored it. "So you just ignored my upstairs/downstairs idea and created a whole new thing? What about my note? Why didn't you at least write back and tell me you were trashing my stuff?"

"What note?" she asks, but not in a nice voice. Not in a nice voice at all. It's a voice that sounds like she doesn't even believe I wrote a note!

I am biting my lip so hard, I'm scared it's going to start bleeding.

Everyone can hear her say in this super-bossy and talking-down way, "Don't worry that you didn't do anything. I got this. Just be quiet and follow my lead."

The texting–nail polish girl in back actually stands up to get a better look at us. I try to stare her down but end up looking away.

I want to pull the other stupid Naomi's hair or pinch her or at least scream really loud, but everyone is already looking at us. Staring at us. Three people are standing now, peering around other people. You'd think that would make me be quiet, but I'm so mad! "I'm not Brianna. You don't get to be a bossy big sister to me."

She keeps playing around with HER project on the screen, and I sit there with my mouth open. Before long I feel Julie standing right in front of us.

"I would like to talk to you both outside the classroom right now."

My stomach ripples with scaredness as we follow Julie into the hall.

"Would one of you like to tell me what's going on?"

I think about starting when we first went to the other Naomi's house for dinner, how we had the same sneakers and Dad forced me to do this class so I'd have to spend more time with her. And then she announced to everyone that she did the whole project without me. But I don't think that's what Julie has in mind.

"We worked together on our project in the beginning, but then SHE got bored," the other Naomi says. "So I finished it myself. And my dad said it was awesome."

Her dad? What does he have to do with anything?

She stands tall and proud, but one look at Julie makes her all slouchy again.

"I have been very clear that this is a team project. A project for a pair to complete together. Do you remember, girls? Collaboration? Mature and generous spirits? Respect? All that is far more important to me, and I hope to you, than the projects themselves." Julie looks right at me. "You were bored with your project?" she asks.

It's too much to explain. "I guess," I say. "Some of it was fun." I can't look her in the eye, but I do make myself say, "I'm sorry. I should have helped more. But when I tried to, she ignored me and did everything by herself."

Julie looks right at the other Naomi now. "If you really did the bulk of the work yourself, or with someone other than your partner, I'm sorry to say that you can't be considered for the showcase." And then she really surprises me by bending over a little and drawing both of us into a hug. "But DuoTek will always be here, you know. Maybe you can get together to work on a project and present it if you join us for the fall session."

As we walk back into the room, I'm almost sure that the other Naomi is doing everything she can to not cry in front of everyone. She doesn't say a thing. She stands as straight as she can and walks back, then slinks into the seat, blinking a lot.

I wish I had made her a costume back when I studied her. She could really use a confident costume right now.

Everyone is looking at us. Every single person. Nail Polish girl is smirking. One girl who was absent for half the class is whispering with the girl next to her.

I want to protect the other Naomi—and maybe myself too—from all the people who turn to stare. But all I can do is sit there and stare back, feeling awful.

CHAPTER TWENTY-THREE

Naomi Marie

"Want my chocolate pudding?" asks Xio. She pats my shoulder. "I think you need it."

I've spent the whole lunch period explaining why we didn't have our "celebration" on Saturday. Explaining that all my hard work didn't even matter to THAT OTHER NAOMI because she is a big lazy babyhead who doesn't do work and gets mad at people who do.

I take the chocolate pudding and the Paddington Bear spoon that Xio is holding out.

"Thanks," I say. "I mean, can you believe her?! I was trying to make us both look good, even though I did EVERYTHING."

Xio nods.

"She called me BOSSY!"

Xio nods.

"I was TRYING to give her some SHINE and not take ALL THE CREDIT even though I DID ALL THE WORK and she just . . . she just . . . was SO MEAN!"

Xio nods.

"Why do you keep nodding?" I ask.

"Because that's what it said you should do in my Friendship Skilz workshop when a BFF is having a crisis and keeps—needs to vent." The bell rings, and Mikey gets busted right as he's about to throw a milk.

"When did you go to that?" I ask, forgetting how mad I am for a second. We start packing up our things and head down the hall to the classroom.

"Um . . . Saturday afternoon. After . . . you know, things didn't happen."

"Oh," I say. Since Mrs. Perkins isn't back yet, we lean on my desk together. "Was it good?"

"Yeah . . . I would have told you, but your mom said you didn't really feel like talking."

"She was right." I do now, though. "And another thing. The game I made by myself? Seriously awesome."

Xio nods, really slowly and exaggerated this time. I start giggling.

"Hey," she says. "Can we make a game together?"

"Sure, that would be way more fun than working with Ms. Evil. I can show you how to use DuoTek."

"Great! Because I have an idea from the Friendship Skilz workshop and *Vocalympians!*"

This time I nod very, very slowly. And we both laugh.

Mrs. Perkins rushes into the classroom and starts talking like she's been there all along. "For this project, you will be working in teams of four. And, yes, I know—one team of five," Mrs. Perkins adds when Margot the Correcter raises her hand. "You'll have ten minutes to work out the teams, and I don't"—she glares at us—"want any nonsense."

Mrs. Perkins never wants any nonsense, and I'm glad. We only have art once a week, and the kids who fool around just mess things up for us all. Last week, Maria V. was my partner, and she drank all the milk with food coloring from our liquid paintings. Mrs. Perkins told us it wasn't poisonous, but since then Maria's been way more annoying than she used to be.

We shuffle around to figure out teams. Xio and Chris Williams jump over to me right away, which gives me a warm, sunshiny feeling; I really need that now.

"Who else?" says Chris, looking around. He tries to make his voice deep and growly. "We must choose wisely."

Xio nudges him. "It's like this. . . ." She clears her throat and growls, "We must choose wisely."

"Whoa!" he says. "How'd you do that?"

"She can go high too," I add. "Like glass breaking."

"I got skills," says Xio. "And I take vocal gymnastics class." She sings what I think is supposed to be a scale, waving her index finger around the whole time. A few people look over, including

Jenn Harlow, who rolls her eyes and whispers to her minions. The same old same old. I swallow the lump that's in my throat and turn away.

"Come on, guys, let's get this done," I say. "I don't want to look like we're slackers."

Yasmine is headed our way, and I smile. She's reliable and not bossy. She'll have this on lock. They'll all see. I can COLLABORATE as good as anyone else. Better, even.

"Come on over, Yazzy," I say. But as she walks toward us, Jenn grabs her arm and drags her away. What's up with that?

"Five minutes!" calls out Mrs. Perkins.

I march over to Jenn's group. "Hey, Yazzy," I say loudly. "Did you want to be on our team?"

She looks at me, then at Jenn. "Um . . ."

Jenn steps forward. "Yazzy's going to be with us," she says. "My friend Drea is in this workshop? Where you make computer games?" Uh-oh. Even though she's ending every sentence with a question mark, we both know exactly where she's going with this. "And she said they had final presentations? And there was this *one* team?" She pauses.

"This one team what?" I ask.

She sighs. "She said it was sooooooo random. This *one* team was the *only one* that didn't show anything, and she felt sooooo sorry for them . . . especially the bossy one who thought she knew everything but was obviously clueless."

I put my hand on my hip, but then I put it down so I don't look that interested. "Really?"

"Yeah, *really*," she says. She rolls her eyes. "Oh, come on, Naomi, you can't play it off. She told me the whole story, and as soon as she described the bossy girl, I knew it was you. And, like, some other girl named Naomi too, which is so weird, like you."

I just keep looking at her, and I don't blink. I can feel my face heat up again as I remember how it felt to be just sitting there doing nothing after all that work. Like I didn't even matter. Again. Like I was being erased. Like I'm not me anymore.

"She said you were trying to cheat or something, and I'm not surprised. That's why I think Yazzy should be with people who do their own work."

I start to say, "I always do my own work!" but I stop. I stand there for another beat so they know that I am me and I am right here. Then I turn and walk away slowly, probably in a way that Momma might call grown. I can hear them whispering behind me.

When I get back to Xio and Chris, they ask what happened. "Jenn is using her powers for evil again," I say, and leave it at that.

Xio raises an eyebrow. "Should I say something?"

"It's no big deal," I say. And it isn't. I know what I did, and what I can do. *Shine your light without dimming anyone else's.* "Come on, we've got like a minute left."

"Maybe we can just be three?" asks Chris. "Or . . ."

We all glance over at Mikey and shudder.

There's a tap on my shoulder, and I turn to see Yazzy.

"Can I work with you guys?" she asks.

I want to ask why, and what about Jenn, but I don't. "Sure," I say. "There's room for one more."

"Thanks," she says. "Jenn thinks everyone should do the work for her. You always have good ideas."

"We've all got skills," I say.

Mrs. Perkins claps. "Time's up. Mikey, if you don't have a team . . ." She looks around the room. "Join Naomi's group." She looks at me like she expects me to complain.

"I like to be called Naomi Marie now, Mrs. Perkins" is all I say.

CHAPTER TWENTY - FOUR

Naomi E.

"So you know how we postponed the celebration because . . ." It would be impossible to sum up how not celebration-y that class with the other Naomi was last weekend, so I let the "because" sit in the air. Birds are singing, and the "because" fades away as they tweet on, mixed in with the sounds of people and cars.

"Yeah," Annie says, watching her feet dribble the soccer ball. She's running some drill she learned at practice that involves kicking the ball high up and then trying to control it with her feet. I always want to say, "It would be so much easier if you'd use your hands," but Annie doesn't find soccer jokes funny.

It's hot this morning, but there are lots of clouds, and when they slide in front of the sun, you can feel a cool breeze too.

Beneath the tree, little not-yet-apricots fell before they had a chance to get ripe, rotting in a sloppy circle around the trunk.

I'm on the swing, rocking slowly, feeling pretty miserable. "I screwed up," I say. I've had that not-hungry-and-then-some feeling in my stomach all week.

Annie's feet keep doing complicated things, but now she's looking up at me. "Yeah? So what really happened?"

I tell her the whole horrible story. Everything. How I kept not doing any work. And how the other Naomi and I argued a lot but sometimes we agreed too, and how some of the stuff we put in our project was really cool. But how in the end it was this whole disaster, and if I had only worked as hard as the other Naomi, everything would have been fine, the class would be over, we'd have had our big celebration, and Annie would have already met the other Naomi.

"I really did want to meet her," Annie says.

I'm almost sure they'd like each other. I can picture Annie "reading" one of Brianna's books, and both of them—Brianna and Naomi—laughing with Annie and me.

"I'm realizing something," I tell Annie. "I actually like her. I was so mad at Dad about everything that I was almost refusing to let her be my friend, you know?"

Incredibly, impossibly, Annie's feet are not moving. The ball is still, right next to her. She's not moving, just waiting, like I've said something she thought she'd never hear.

"She's really smart. And kind of funny too."

I wish I could make this better. And without thinking too

much about it, I say, "So I have this idea"—even though it's only the start of one—"and maybe you could meet her."

"I'm tired of waiting. When? When would I meet her?"

"Now?"

I don't exactly lie to my dad, because it is true, as I said, that we're heading toward Annie's now. I don't mention that we'll be walking right past her house after we head toward it. Annie and I are barely on our way when she asks, "Exactly how mad will your dad be if he finds out?"

Good question. Hard to answer. "He won't find out," I tell her. I want to say more, but the loudest bus in the history of transportation is right next to us. It could win awards for snorty and groaning loudness. We walk faster to get away, but it catches up to us. Annie stops, turns, and gives it a nasty look. A bus! When it finally turns, we can hear each other again.

"We're allowed to walk to each other's houses all the time, right?" I say.

Annie looks at me like she's not even going to bother answering such a stupid question. "It's the other part," she says. "Are you allowed to walk to the Y yourself?"

She knows I'm not. All because of one stupid street. That very wide street we have to cross where there was once a terrible accident and so now I need to be with my dad to cross, probably until I graduate high school. Or maybe even after that. "I walked there every week with my dad for the six stupid classes," I say. And then, remembering I'm trying to be nicer about the whole DuoTek thing, I say, "For six whole weeks."

Annie makes a face at me—eyebrows raised, half a smile—that says, *You totally didn't answer my question, and we both know you are not allowed to cross that street without an adult.*

We're a block from Annie's when she stops walking. She looks at me, confused, and says, "So wait a minute. You know her schedule by heart? You're sure the other Naomi will be there now?"

I shake my head. "But she made it sound like she's always there. Like she practically owns the building. She takes swimming, African dance, and probably five other things too. And if she's not there, maybe she'll be at the library."

"Our library?"

"Um, no, I don't think so, but we could figure it out. I'm sure we'll find her. I need to at least try. I want to, you know, talk it out. And tell her I'm sorry."

When we reach Annie's house, she races to the end of the lawn to grab a new ball because her soccer feet need it, and she's almost all the way back to the sidewalk when her mom opens the front door. "Naomi! Annie, I thought you were staying at Naomi's today."

Annie is the worst liar. This hardly ever comes up—the only time I saw it was one huge lie about Halloween candy she was supposed to share with her brothers. But it's like she's playing freeze tag. Right here on the sidewalk, Annie has stopped walking, dribbling, talking. My best friend the statue.

Not that *I* know exactly how to handle this. I wasn't counting on parents.

"Are you staying here now? Naomi, should I call your father?" her mom asks.

"NO!" I say—too loud and too fast, and just way too *too*.

"We were about to . . ." Maybe she won't notice that it's not a complete sentence.

Her mom looks. And looks. And finally says, "Well, Annie, since you're home, you may as well come with me to pick up Chase. I was going to call now anyway. We can give you a lift if you'd like, Naomi."

"No thanks," I say. I should probably say more, but maybe saying less is the way to go with . . . lying. I don't have a ton of experience. I wave and smile and keep walking, even though maybe it's a little weird that I'm heading in the opposite direction of home.

When I reach Scary Boulevard, I'm thinking about what I want to say to Naomi. I know I at least owe it to my dad to cross at the corner, wait at the light, and be as careful as I can be. And I am. It's no big deal, really. It's not like I'm six. I can cross big streets. This shouldn't even be something I have to worry about my father getting mad about.

As I walk up to the Y, I'm trying to remember if there's a directory about which class meets in which room. And—uh-oh—did all classes end the same week as Girls Gaming the System? Is this the stupidest idea ever? I brace myself for the awful smell and walk in, hoping I'll figure it out, and suddenly there's someone wet wrapped around my waist, jumping up and down and saying, "White Naomi! White Naomi! What are you doing here?"

Valerie turns the corner from the other hallway, saying, "Brianna, don't run—" and then she sees me and says, "Naomi! What are you doing here?"

The question of the day! Which I answer with a question of my own. "Is Naomi here? I wanted to talk to her."

I wish I had a stopwatch so I could tell you exactly how long Valerie stands there staring at me. I also wish I had a towel, because Brianna is getting me soaked! She finally unhugs and takes a step back and looks at me the same way her mother does.

Valerie's shaking her head as she asks, "Is your father here?"

"No," I say.

She tilts her head a little and then asks, "Does he know you're here?"

This is bad. "Not exactly," I say.

"And the reason you're here but he doesn't know is . . . ?"

This is very bad. "I wanted to talk to Naomi. I had a feeling she'd be here."

Brianna keeps looking back and forth between us. Her mouth is wide open.

Valerie holds her phone. "Do you want to call your dad or do you want me to?"

I don't want either of those things.

CHAPTER TWENTY-FIVE

Naomi Marie

It's one thing being the New Naomi Marie when I don't have to see Ms. E(vil); it's not so easy when we're on our way to meet her for the first time since she made me look stupid in front of everyone.

"Please don't pout, Naomi Marie," says Momma. "It's over. Let it go."

"Easy for you to say. *You* weren't completely destroyed in front of the whole world."

Momma raises her eyebrow and turns to me as we walk to the parking lot. "Destroyed? The whole world? Don't you think you're being a little dramatic?"

"Drama Queeeen, you're a super-fiend," sings Xio under her breath. She flinches when I glare at her. "Sorry. It's just one of George Henderson's verses on Adedayo's—" She stops. "Never mind."

Momma unlocks the car door, and we all buckle up.

"We should have just canceled, not postponed," I say. I've been very happy to not think about last Saturday all week. Now every mortifying moment is coming back in a rush like a waterfall. "There's nothing to celebrate about that . . . that . . . debbuckle. Let's just forget the whole thing. Can't we just go to the park by ourselves?"

"You mean *de-BAH-cle*, honey," Momma says softly, looking back and smiling.

Humph. I thought that sounded weird. I fold my arms and look out of the window as we get onto the highway.

"I liked what you made," Momma says. "I don't want to forget it. And neither do you. Maybe you can do a presentation at school or something."

"Don't say 'presentation'! *And* we missed the showcase deadline. We were the . . . the Fools Not Gaming the System!"

"Fool's gold never gets old . . . ," sing Xio and Bri. I turn to them.

"Sorry," says Xio. "It's just, not many people say 'fools,' . . . and also, that was one of—"

"ADEDAYO! I know, I know," I say. "How do *you* know that song?" I ask Brianna.

"I know everything," she answers. "I have graduation soon." Then she turns it into a song. "I have graaaad-yooooo-A-shun SOOOOOON!"

I cover my ears and turn back to the window.

"Hey," says Momma gently. "We're celebrating your hard work, that you tried a new thing. We're going to your favorite park, and we even got your favorite Zipcar!"

"It doesn't even smell new anymore," I grumble. "That's what I hate about Zipcars—everybody uses them, and then they get old."

Momma glances at me in the rearview mirror but just keeps driving.

"I bet there's a way to make this fun," whispers Xio. "You know you always come up with something. Do you have any game ideas?"

Xio's got my back. I try to smile as I shrug. "Forget it. It's not a big deal."

She squeezes my hand, and I add, "Thanks."

As we head across the bridge, Brianna spots another Zipcar in the lane next to us and waves. The driver doesn't wave back, so I stick out my tongue on my sister's behalf, and that makes me feel a tiny bit better.

My best friend is here.

We're going to my favorite park, in a Zipcar.

With a picnic cooler full of treats.

And I WILL NEVER HAVE TO COLLABORATE AND

COOPERATE WITH THE OTHER NAOMI AGAIN.

I guess there's still plenty to celebrate.

We get to the park first, and the sprinklers are on, so me, Xio, and Bri start running through the one shaped like an octopus. When Momma and Dad were getting divorced, I got to use some "take a break days" and skip school; I asked to come here every time. You can do things like run through the sprinklers without wondering if someone's mom is going to complain loudly about "big kids" being too rough.

Kids are already wearing shorts and flip-flops, and screaming like someone just announced a free lifetime supply of ice cream for everyone. We've got a few more weeks of school left, but this park always makes me feel like summer. I can breathe deeper near the river; it's like I put my problems on one of the little boats leaving the harbor, far away and getting farther by the minute.

"Tom!" Momma yells, waving frantically and smiling.

They're here. Yay. Tom smiles and starts heading toward us. Naomi Edith is being draggy behind him. Another girl, who I guess must be Annie, is kind of walking between them, looking like she doesn't know how she's supposed to look.

Tom flops down on our blanket. "Ugh, it feels like the middle of summer already!" he says. "I packed sunscreen!"

He looks a little red already. Momma must agree, because she says, "I'll help you with that," which is my cue to run far, far away. I can feel Xio and Bri running with me, but when I turn to them, it's *her*.

I slow down.

"Hi," she says. "You run pretty fast."

"I'm in the Mighty Milers club," I say.

"I'm not," she says, bending over. "I'm more in the Super Sitters."

She looks up like she's hoping I'm going to laugh.

"So . . . how was your week? I mean, after . . ." She clears her throat.

"The total fail?" I finish. "The complete mortification?" I guess I'm still a little upset. I look around to make sure Xio's not close enough to hear me.

"Well, I was just going to say kind of bad," she says. "But, um, okay, if you want to go in that direction . . ."

"Why did you have to say anything?" I ask. "It was YOUR idea to work together. Then you didn't want to help at all! And after I did all the work, and I did a good job too, if I do say so myself—"

"You'll definitely say so yourself," she says, but I keep going.

"I did a GREAT job, and then you had to go and mess it up in front of Julie and everyone!" I take a deep breath. "And my dad was going to come, but he didn't because of YOUR dad, and—"

Then the worst happens. I start crying.

And so does she.

Bri comes running up. "Are you guys playing tag? Because if you are— Oh Naomis, are you crying?" She looks really worried as Xio and Annie come up behind her.

"Um, Bri, let's go back to the sprinklers, okay?" says Xio.

"Yeah!" says Annie quickly. "I'll show you how my flip-flops change colors when they get wet!" They both grab Bri by the hand on each side and hustle her away.

After a while, the Other Naomi says, "Xiomara seems cool."

"It's just 'Xio' now. . . . Annie seems cool too." We lean against a tree and watch them play with Brianna. A few pigeons wander over, but they stalk away once they realize we don't have any snacks.

"I'm sorry," we both say at the exact same time.

Then we laugh. And laugh, and laugh, until we're both laid out on the grass, looking up at the sky.

"It's so funny how you can be crying one minute and then laughing the next, right?" I say.

"I know!" she says. "My mom says—" Then she stops.

"How's your mom?" I ask after minute. And before she even lifts a shoulder, I add, "And don't SHRUG!"

"You really do have this bossy-big-sister thing down, don't you?" she says. And we giggle until she almost whispers, "I miss her."

I lie really still, like she's a deer that might run away if I move too fast.

"And I thought I would have visited her by now and we hardly get to Skype and I used to be able to talk to my mom whenever I wanted but now I never get what I want and everything's already decided before I even realize what I want."

She says that all in one breath.

It's a risk, but . . . "You sure do sound like an only child," I say. She looks at me for a beat, and then she laughs. Whew.

"Hey, did you notice the weather?" I ask.

"Huh?"

"It's not raining."

"You're right," she says. "That's a good sign."

We're silent for a while.

"Did you like that class?" she asks.

It's my turn to shrug. "It was okay. At first, I was really like NO. It was not how I planned to spend my Saturday mornings. But . . . it got kind of interesting. And when I tried making my own project, I . . . I showed it to my dad, and he got really into it, and it was like how we do puzzles and board games together, but we never have that much time now. . . ." I trail off. "Anyway, I always figure if I have to do something, I might as well make it good."

"You mean make it THE BEST," she says. "You're kind of competitive."

"I just want to do MY best," I say.

"I guess my ideas weren't up to par," she says.

"What ideas?"

"The ones I put in the Brain Dump," she says. "About the stairs and stuff?"

"I never saw that," I say slowly. "Is that the note you were talking about? I sent you some messages in the Dump and you never answered, so I stopped checking after a while."

"Ohhh . . ." She nods like I've just explained the mysteries of the universe to her. "Well, do you think maybe you gave up on me too soon?"

". . . Maybe. But do you think maybe you didn't exactly give me that much to work with? Like, ideas that stayed 'in your head'? I mean, I know I'm magic, but . . ."

We look at each other for a while. I bite my lip, and then she bites hers. A giggle escapes and I clap my hand over my mouth, but it's too late. We're both laughing again.

Bri runs over. "THEY STOPPED CRYING," she yells over to Xio and Annie, who are sitting on the swings.

"They look like friends," says the Other Naomi, watching them walk over to us.

"We have good taste," I say.

We play Lava Monster together until we hear the ice cream truck. We all look at each other.

"What do you think? Should we ask?" says the Other Naomi. "We brought a lot of good stuff from Morningstar."

"It IS supposed to be a celebration," I say. "But we brought Shelly Ann's triple-chocolate cake too."

"We'll ask," says Xio. "Parents always say yes to the guests."

"I like the way you think," says Annie. The two of them head toward Momma and Tom, while the Other Naomi and I take turns pushing Bri on the swings.

Xio and Annie come back, and they're not smiling.

"What's wrong?" I ask.

"The ice cream man left!" cries Bri, looking around. "That's what's wrong."

"Um. Well, no, that's not it," says Annie, looking at Xio. "It's, um, well . . ."

Xio's looking back at Annie, and both of their eyebrows are about to leap off their heads. Then they start signaling to each other in fake sign language like the rest of us aren't even there, and this is so silly that both the Other Naomi and I say "WHAT?!?!" at the same time. And laugh.

Annie starts. "It's just . . . your parents—"

"—they were really looking at each other," blurts out Xio.

"So?" says the Other Naomi.

"Xio, you know Momma believes in eye contact," I say.

"I mean *really* looking," says Xio. "Like on those book covers in the teen section." She turns to Annie. "Which is the only section that looks interesting."

"I know, right?" says Annie.

The Other Naomi and I share an eye roll.

"They keep holding hands," says Annie.

My stomach hurts.

"And touching foreheads," adds Xio.

Wait, no, it's my head.

"They're doing it now!" shouts Bri.

MY EYES.

We all watch for a while, and it's pretty gross. I mean, it kind of always is, but . . .

The air is gone. I can't breathe. What happened to the air?

"They're *in love*," Annie whispers. The Other Naomi opens her mouth like she wants to say something, but nothing comes out.

"Your mouth is open," Bri says to me. "But nothing's coming out. You're gonna catch flies in there!"

"Be quiet, Bri," the Other Naomi whispers, just as I was about to.

"Yeah, Bri," I say. "Just be quiet."

CHAPTER TWENTY-SIX

Naomi E.

"Bessie, this must be your lucky day," Sheera says as we walk into Morningstar.

Morningstar!

It smells so good. There's a coffee smell, of course, but also baking bread and sweet chocolaty things and all-around goodness. Oh my. So good. But maybe better—getting hugged by Bessie. "How has it happened that I'm never here when you are anymore? Look at you! I bet you've grown two inches!"

"Hello? I'm here too," Dad says.

"Yes, you are, Tom," Sheera says. "But Bessie missed Naomi more."

I doubt I could smile any bigger. This is exactly what I need.

Everything has felt so wrong since Dad and Valerie got all . . .
gross at the park. And before that, a different version of awful,
with Dad mad at me for going to the Y.

"So what will it be, miss," Bessie asks. "Croissant or bagel?"

Would you believe I can't choose? Like, seriously can't?
Bessie starts laughing. Sheera says, "Now, come on! Do you want
both? Because I can make that happen."

Finally, I hear myself say, "Chocolate chip scone, please."

Dad starts slow-clapping. "Change!" he says. "Change is
good!"

"I don't know about that," Sheera says. "But I do know our
scones are good."

Bessie takes off her apron and sits with Dad and me. She
tells me about her little dog, Kerfluffle. She shows me at least
seventeen pictures on her phone. She asks about Mom and says,
"Oh, good!" and gives me a one-armed hug when I tell her
Mom will be home for a whole month.

Dad sips tea and listens. I find myself telling Bessie about the
whole mess with the DuoTek project and how things were pretty
bad between the other Naomi and me but are now getting better.
I skip over the part where Valerie called Dad and waited for him
to show up at the Y to walk me home, when we had the first of
about four billion conversations about street safety and trust. I
jump ahead to how we had a There Are Plenty of Other Things
to Celebrate get-together in the park with my friend Annie and
Naomi's friend Xio and I definitely skip over the disgusting Dad-
and-Valerie part.

A few people are waiting for coffee, and Sheera holds up Bessie's apron. "Break's over," Bessie says. "But it sounds like you have an awful lot to look forward to. I'm happy to hear that."

Before we leave, Dad lets me pick out cookies, which is very happy making. Maybe we're finally getting back to normal. I hope I can still recognize normal.

There are a dozen in the box when Dad says, "Whoa, whoa, whoa. That's a lot of cookies for three people."

"Three?"

"Valerie's coming over."

First of all, he is so wrong about that being a lot of cookies. Because even if it were three people, that's four cookies each, and that's not a lot. Math, Dad! But why isn't he counting us? Am I supposed to watch Valerie, Brianna, and the other Naomi eat cookies?

"Five," I say. "Five people." And then, turning back to Sheera, I say, "And two of the butterscotch chip, please, and do you have that one with chocolate sprinkles?"

"We're out," she says.

"That's plenty, thanks, Sheera," Dad says. "It's only Val coming today," he says.

"No Naomi or Brianna?"

"That's right," Dad says. He walks to the cash register, where Stefan rings everything up. When Dad's busy counting out dollars, Sheera hands me a frosted brownie in a sneaky, don't-let-your-dad-see way. "I missed you," she whispers.

I smile at her, wondering why tears are making a surprise

attack in my eyes. I look down and say, "Me too."

"Let's go, Naomi," Dad says, and so we do.

As we're walking home, I ask, "Why is just Valerie coming over?"

Dad stops walking and looks at me, so I stop too. "What?" I ask.

"Is there a reason you don't want Valerie to come over? You know she had to tell me about you showing up at the Y, right? Any responsible adult would have told me."

Hoo, boy.

"That's not what I meant," I say. I don't say, *Because it's not like we haven't had this* you betrayed my trust, Naomi *conversation enough times to last my whole life.* "It's just that every time I've seen her we've also seen her kids, right? At their house, at our house, every Saturday." My voice catches when I say that last part. Like a little leak of all the stuff I had been holding inside.

"Come with me," Dad says, motioning to the park across the street. But we don't even go in. We sit on a bench outside the entrance, between two big trees.

"Talk to me," Dad says.

"What?" I say.

"Talk."

"It's not a big deal," I say. "I was surprised it was only Valerie, because it's never been only Valerie."

"Huh. I don't even think I realized that," he says, sounding a little surprised. "Because I see Valerie, just the two of us, sometimes; but it's when you're doing other things—sleeping over at Grandma and Grandpa's or spending time at Annie's—so okay. But were you almost crying when you mentioned Girls Gaming the System? I know it didn't end well and that you were mad about me signing you up without consulting you, but is there something else?"

Even though we already talked about it a billion times and it didn't feel like such a big deal when I did it, I'm still embarrassed and filled with guilt about doing something I wasn't allowed to do and it all bursts right to the surface in a big fat hurry and I'm crying and can't really talk and then I'm shaking my head because I can't even believe this. It's over and we already talked about it, but I can't stop myself from being a whole crying mess on a park bench in front of the whole world.

"I really don't know what this is," I say. My feelings seem to be carrying on without me somehow. Maybe sometimes the sad sticks around longer than you think it should.

"What time is Valerie coming over?" I ask, wiping away the stupid tears. He gasps and looks at his watch. Then he grabs my hand and we start to run.

When we reach our house, she's not there yet. But before I'm even done washing my hands in the bathroom, I hear Dad talking to Valerie, and then, ugh, it's quiet, and I guess he's kissing her. I dry my hands and take a deep breath.

"Hi," I say, as friendly as I ever am, when I walk into what's probably always going to feel like Mom's sewing room since Dad and I haven't done anything to change it into any other kind of room. Dad steps into the kitchen.

Valerie and I look at each other for a second too long, and I wish someone would say something like *So this feels awkward, doesn't it?* Because maybe then we could laugh or joke about it, but instead we share the awkward.

"I wanted to see you," she says. "So we could talk about what happened." Which is a terrible way to start. "And also, I brought you something." That right there is a much better way to A) get my attention, and B) break up awkwardness of any kind.

"That was nice of you," I say, hoping it's something delicious. But it's a book, with a bow on it.

"Have you read this?" she asks.

"I've never seen it," I say. "What's it about?"

"Sisters. It's a beautiful book, but I don't mean that in the way some teachers do, because it's also a joy to read. And I thought that if I could give you a little something, Naomi, I would like that to be joy."

There is really and truly something wrong with the tears in my body today. They keep thinking it's time to cry when it's really not. I eke out the words *thank you*. And then I make myself say, "And I understand why you had to tell my dad." I don't add the words *kind of*, but it's possible I think them a little.

Valerie looks at me and then looks away, like she doesn't want to embarrass me maybe, and then she starts talking again. "I understand. Thank you for saying that."

"And thank *you* for not bringing it up in front of everyone at the park. What did Naomi Marie say when you told her?"

"I didn't," Valerie says. I think we're finally done discussing this, but then she adds, "I thought we'd keep it between us."

It takes a huge effort to keep myself from pointing out that there's no way Brianna didn't tell Naomi Marie the minute they got home. But I somehow manage to keep my mouth shut. And so does Valerie.

I'm afraid the quiet is going to keep growing, but then Valerie says, "What I especially like about this book is that each of the sisters is unique. Her very own person. And the sisters' dedication to each other is fierce."

Dad starts to walk into the room, but Valerie gives him some secret eye message that sends him back into the kitchen.

"Are Brianna and your Naomi fierce like that?"

Valerie turns to me like I've asked a really thoughtful question. "In some ways. I expect there will be more of that as they get older."

"I like being an only child," I say. "But I've always wondered about sisters."

"Interesting," Valerie says.

CHAPTER TWENTY – SEVEN

Naomi Marie

Momma kisses my forehead. "Those were the best waffles you've ever made!"

"The bestest best ever!" sings Bri, throwing out her hands and knocking over my homemade brown sugar syrup. But I don't even mind.

Tom eats his last piece. "Delicious, Naomi Marie. Maybe you can give me your recipe."

"NO, DAD!" says the Other Naomi quickly. "I don't think you should try this at home." She looks at me and smiles. "They were probably the best waffles I ever ate, but I think ... they're *your* special recipe, right? I'd rather have them whenever we come see you." She raises her eyebrows. "My dad might ... do something different."

"Oh yeah!" I say. "It's my treat. It can always be my treat."

Tom pretends to pout. "Is this a comment on my cooking abilities?"

"Yes!" we all say, and laugh.

But as we clean up, I whisper to the Other Naomi, "I can teach YOU how to make them if you want."

"I'd like that," she says. "Thanks." She points to my sundress. "That's so pretty, all those blues and yellows. Is it tie-dyed?"

I hold the skirt out around me like I'm fancy. "Sort of. I went to a class at the natural history museum, and they taught us how to do this kind of dyeing called adire the way it's done in Nigeria. We took the fabric I worked on and made this dress." She's a little dressed up today too. "I like *your* skirt," I say.

"My mom sent it," she says, twirling a little. "It's vintage. I would never have thought I'd wear something so . . . twirly, but I really like it. I added the flower."

"There's this book I have on hold at the library. It's instructions for making your old clothes into new ones. It finally came in. Do you want to go to the library with me to pick it up?"

"Sure!" she says. We go to ask the parents, who say, "Of course!" and look like we just gave them a million dollars. Adults always have to make a big deal out of EVERYTHING.

"I need to help Bri de-syrup," says Momma. She looks at Tom.

"I have to run a couple of errands," he says.

"We can walk," I say quickly. "It's not far."

"Do you girls promise not to jaywalk, even if there aren't any cars coming?"

I look at Naomi. She looks back. I mean, parents!

"Promise out loud, please," Momma says.

"Momma, we've got this," I say. "Seriously."

"Yeah," says Naomi. "I've learned my lesson."

"You sure have," says Bri.

"What are you guys talking about?" I ask.

"I'll tell you later," says Naomi.

"I won't, because I promised, and I kept my promise good this time!" says Bri.

"Okay, okay," Momma says. "We'll meet you girls there. We have . . . a surprise to share later."

"ICE CREAM!" yells Bri. "CAKE!"

"Can we go to Shelly Ann's?" I ask.

"Or Morningstar?" Naomi asks.

"Just go ahead to the library," says Momma. "We'll figure it out."

"Figure it out, figure it out, Naomi Marie and Naomi E.," sings Bri. "Listen, you rhyme!"

"See you later, girls," says Tom. "I'm just going to finish up a few things in the kitchen before I head out. Valerie, I'll swing back by here and pick you and Syrup Girl up, then we can head over to the library to get the girls."

"I'll be ready in a minute. I just have to do something," I say to Naomi.

"I'll meet you out front," she says.

I follow Tom into the kitchen. He's wiping the table down, and even though it's pretty weird to see him so comfortable in here, I notice that he's using the right spray, the one that smells like grapefruit.

"Tom?" I start, then stop. He looks at me and smiles.

"What's up, Naomi Marie?"

"Um . . . thank you . . . thank you for respecting my dad, and me, and . . . everything."

He's still for a minute, then he nods. "It's my pleasure. I'm glad you're all a part of my life. You're a gift."

I like thinking of myself as a gift.

"And . . . thank you for maybe taking us *out* to eat in the future," I add.

He laughs and holds up his hand for a high five, so I give it. And when he takes my hand and squeezes it, I let him.

Ms. Starr looks up from trying to tape together *Viva Frida*. "I think this is hopeless," she says. "Would you like to use it for one of your projects, Naomi? Such great colors. A collage, maybe?" She glances at the Other Naomi and smiles. "Hello."

"Sure, thanks, Ms. Starr," I say. "And I forgot to tell you—I'm being called Naomi Marie now." I stand a little straighter. "I think it's more elegant, don't you?"

"Oh, I do," she says. "And that suits you for sure. What's *your* elegant name?" she says to the Other Naomi.

"Oh! Sorry," I say. "This is, um, my . . . friend. Naomi E."

Ms. Starr blinks for a minute, then grins. "Two Naomis! In my library! I am a lucky lady."

A boy comes to the desk with every volume of the Bone

series. I think that's so not fair to take them all out at once like that, but I don't say anything. I look around and am surprised to see that the computers are free.

"Where's Teen Gamez Crew?" I ask.

"Field trip," answers Ms. Starr. "To the GameLife arcade. They're coming a little later."

"Can we get on the DuoTek site here?" I ask. "It's a coding site for kids."

"And collaboration and cooperation," Naomi E. adds, and we giggle.

"I'm sure you can," says Ms. Starr.

I look at Naomi E. "Are you thinking what I'm thinking?"

"No," she says.

"Remember what Julie said? DuoTek will always be here. . . . We can work on it on our own time."

"Seriously?"

"I'm kind of interested in your stairs idea. . . ." I wiggle my eyebrows.

"Really?"

"Yes, really. Doing my best also means being open to suggestions, you know."

She looks at me for a long minute, then says, "Lead the way."

"I knew you'd go for it," I say. "Actually . . ." I pull a folded piece of paper from my pocket and hand it to her. "Here."

"What's this?"

"My list . . . about you." Suddenly I feel shy. "Like . . . the good things."

"It doesn't look very long," she says, smiling. Then she's quiet as she reads. After a minute she looks up.

"You think I'm creative? And . . . authentic?"

I nod. "You keep it real."

"And have good taste in clothes?"

"Also excellent taste in friends," I say. "And you understand important things, like cake and good books."

"Can I keep this?" she asks.

"Sure," I say. "I won't forget it."

We pull two chairs over to one computer, which Ms. Starr says is okay since it's a Two-Naomi Special Occasion. Before we start, Naomi E. says, "What you said about being called Naomi Marie, are you really okay with that?"

I nod. "It's all good. It reminds me of . . . the fullness of love." Maybe one day I'll tell her about Marie. "And it really is elegant."

We get to work. We each take turns writing a line of code, and it's like we're writing this really fun choose-your-own-adventure type of story together. We put in cats, dogs, the Afro-puff ballerina, and a girl with a blue ponytail. And a big purple whale! We create a park for them (with a big lake for the whale, which Naomi E. says doesn't make sense but I say we can do whatever we want in games so I convince her to leave it). We add music, and make a click-and-drag part so that our characters can pack a picnic lunch consisting entirely of cakes and cookies! We're having fun, and I'm really surprised when I look up and realize that there are people standing behind us, watching.

The Teen Gamez Crew.

"Oh—sorry," I say. "We were just using them while you guys were gone."

"No, don't stop!" says the one who helped me get a book from a high shelf once.

"This looks cool! What game is this? We just saw all the latest ones at GameLife, but I don't remember this."

"Uh, it's not out yet," I say.

"Actually," says Naomi E., "it's pretty exclusive. We're still in development mode. You're getting a first look." She smiles at me.

A big grin spreads across my face. "Yeah, sorry, we're going to have to shut it down now. It's . . . *proprietary* stuff." I hope that was the right word.

"Are you saying *you* made this?" says a girl who laughed at me once when I was handing out So Sewy flyers. "You know how to program?"

"You should join the Teen Gamez Crew," says the first kid. "Sometimes we make exceptions for kids your age." He looks over at Brandon Davis, who is staring at our game in a way that totally makes up for that terrible Presentation Day. "And the ones we have now can't even do stuff like this."

"Thanks, but that's okay," I say, shutting down the computer. "Maybe you can join my club. *Our* club. We don't just *play* games, though. We're about being creators, not just consumers."

Naomi E. nods.

"Where's your flyer?" says the girl who's not laughing now.

"Oh," I say, thinking fast. "We don't do flyers. You can just see Ms. Starr at the desk. She'll take your information . . ."

"And we'll get back to you," says Naomi E.

"Part of the application process," I say.

Some of them roll their eyes, but a couple of them nod, including the nice one who might be cute if I thought boys were cute, but since I don't I'll just say he's a nice high-shelf helper.

As they drift away, I whisper to Naomi E., "Thanks for having my back. Let's go tell Ms. Starr so she knows what's going on."

"So are you really going to start a club?" Naomi E. asks.

"Yes . . . sort of. I mean, will you do it with me?"

She stares at me. "But I—well—this isn't my library. . . ."

"I think you'll be here a lot," I say. "When you're hanging with me. And Xio. And Annie, if you want. We can do the meetings then."

She thinks for a minute. "Are you asking, or telling, Naomi Marie?"

"I'm asking if you want to try it, and telling you that it's a good idea, Naomi E.," I say. "And . . . maybe we can do something together at your library? Or someplace else you love?"

She nods slowly. "Maybe . . . yeah, that might be fun."

And I believe that now—it really might.

We both smile. Big smiles.

We cross our arms and shake hands. Then we go tell Ms. Starr the news.

CHAPTER TWENTY-EIGHT

Naomi E.

"Your library's pretty cool," I say. "But it would be even better if they let us eat in there."

She looks at me in a way that makes me think I proved myself to be an even better person than she ever imagined. "Exactly!" she says.

Dad and Valerie are smiling as they watch us say good-bye to Ms. Starr. Brianna spots us and starts wiggling and jumping up and down, covering her mouth like she can barely hold her words in. As we get closer, she uncovers her mouth and starts whisper-singing the word *surprise* as though it has five syllables.

"Sorry," Naomi Marie says, not sounding sorry at all. "This is not a surprise. We knew you'd all be here."

Brianna doesn't stop mini-jumping but says, "That's not the surprise!"

Valerie says, "Brianna doesn't know what the surprise is. She simply knows there *is* a surprise."

When we step outside, a strong breeze blows Brianna's braids around her face. She swats them away and sings, "Where are we going? Where's my surprise?"

"It's not your surprise, Brianna," Valerie says.

"We're getting a Zipcar later! Surprise!" Brianna says. "See? I kept the secret," she says to her mom.

"Why do we need a car?" I ask.

"Are we going back to the park?" Naomi Marie asks. I think about how we screamed at each other until we cried there. But then we laughed and laughed. Still, I wish I could go back a few weeks and be a better DuoTek partner to Naomi Marie. I know I already apologized, but I keep thinking about it. I don't like how I acted.

Dad and Valerie share a look and say, "Let's talk." I wonder if the only surprise is that we're getting a Zipcar today or if there may be some chocolate in my future.

"This is a big moment for all of us," Dad says.

Valerie reaches for her girls' hands and then looks at me with an expression that says *I wish I had another hand, but I don't.* Dad puts his hands on my shoulders like we're playing a sport or something and coming up with our game plan. Then they make a weird effort to join our two strange circles, but instead we're standing next to each other with my hip touching Naomi

Marie's. We must look crazy to anyone watching.

"Right here, right now," Valerie says. "We are all going to always remember this."

Incredibly, Brianna doesn't start singing the words *right here, right now*.

"We're getting married," Valerie says, smiling. Naomi Marie's mouth opens a little, but no sound comes out. Brianna breaks out of their hand-holding family circle and starts shouting, "Wedding! Wedding! Flower girl! I'm flower girl because I'm youngest!"

"Really?" I say. "Wow. I didn't think. I . . . I didn't know."

"How is that even possible?" Naomi Marie asks. "We don't have enough rooms—and they don't . . . How could we all fit?"

"We've been looking together for a while now, and we think we've found the perfect place for us to all move into together. We want to show it to you! It's a beautiful house—a warm butter yellow, with a backyard and a little garden on the side."

"Can we get a pony?" Brianna asks, and somehow, instead of that being annoying, it makes me and Naomi Marie start to laugh.

But it's just a quick laugh, and then my brain creeps back to this news. A wedding, all of us living together. I had no idea this could happen so fast.

"When will the wedding be?" Naomi Marie asks in a very quiet voice.

"In about a half hour," Tom says.

"WHAT!?" Naomi Marie and I say at the exact same time.

"We got our marriage license last week," Dad explains.

I am pretty sure if I ask why it's happening so fast, that will be considered rude. So I'm very relieved when Naomi Marie asks, "Why's it happening so fast?"

"We didn't want a big wedding," Valerie says. "We had been planning to do it in the fall, and last week we realized this summer would be a great chance for us to all be together as a family. And then that house showed up, and it felt like a sign; there was no reason to wait. All we want, all we really need, is to have you three girls with us."

That's a lot to think about. But then I think of the really important question that hasn't even been mentioned. "But what about wedding cake?"

Everyone laughs, and then Dad says, "Let's get going. The office closes at four thirty."

We start to walk toward City Hall.

Before we even reach the corner, Brianna starts singing, "Momma and Tom sitting in a tree, *K-I-S-S-I-N-G*. First comes love, then comes marriage, then—"

"Brianna, please stop," Naomi Marie and I say—at the exact same time, of course.

"Oh great," Brianna says. "Now I'm going to have two big sisters named Naomi telling me when to stop and what to do."

Sisters! These girls are going to be my sisters? In a half hour? There should be some special quiet-space building we could go to and all sit and think about this before we march over to City Hall.

Naomi Marie says, "Naomi E. asked an important question. What about wedding cake?"

"We thought of that," Dad says.

"When we leave the city clerk's office, we're going straight to the bakery."

"Shelly Ann's?" I ask, trying to keep the disappointment out of my voice.

"Morningstar?" Naomi Marie asks.

"Which one?!" Brianna asks. "I want Shelly Ann's!"

"Well, that's the thing," Dad says.

Valerie stops walking and turns so she's facing the three of us. "It's not going to be this or that, girls. We promise you that. We're bringing two families together. It's not about choosing one. It's very much going to be this AND that. The traditions of both our families, celebrated and honored together."

"I don't get it," Brianna says.

"I think she means Shelly Ann's *and* Morningstar," I say.

"Two bakeries? In one day?" Brianna asks.

"And then we're going to get our car and drive up to Bear Mountain for a big picnic dinner," Dad says.

Naomi Marie doesn't say anything, but her eyes are open very wide. As we start walking again, I'm worried that she's going to say something about not wanting to live with Dad and me. I'm not sure that what I'd choose would be to live with these two girls and their mom, but I can see it's what is going to happen. Like when Mom and Dad got divorced—it was happening, and there was no changing it. I need more time to think about this, but I do like the idea of *and* instead of *or*.

"So there *will* be some chocolate on this day," I say, because it's what jumps to my mind. And it makes me happy.

Naomi Marie smiles, a small one. "Probably a lot," she says.

In the city clerk's office, Brianna sings for everyone in the waiting area, and Valerie shows Naomi Marie and me pictures of the small, perfect wedding cake waiting for us at Morningstar and Shelly Ann's caramel cake decorated with a bride, groom, and three smaller people standing on top.

It's a super-fast ceremony, Dad looking into Valerie's eyes and Valerie into Dad's, all of them wet with tears. It isn't easy to watch—because even though it's not about her at all, I keep thinking about my mom—but I do. I watch the whole thing.

And when Naomi Marie reaches for my hand, I squeeze hers gently. I hope that's what sisters do.

When the ceremony is over, we stand together in a five-person hug back in the waiting area. Ten minutes ago, I was an only child. Now I have two sisters.

Outside, I spot Dad's friend Loofie with his camera. I run over to hug him. "You missed it," I say. "They already got married."

His camera's hanging around his neck, but he holds it up and says, "I'm here to take pictures."

I look down—so do Naomi Marie and Brianna. "But we don't have fancy clothes," Brianna says, sounding sad.

"That's the point," Valerie says. "We wanted some pictures

of us at the start, as we are, as we begin our lives together."

We crowd together with City Hall behind us, and Loofie starts snapping.

I think the other Naomi and I see it at the exact same time. "Wait a minute," I say as she is saying, "Be back in a sec."

I'm glad I grabbed that ten dollars I found in my sock drawer this morning.

There's a man with a small cart selling bouquets of flowers. We race over and then stop, look at each other, and laugh.

"What's your mother's favorite color?" I ask.

"Momma says she doesn't have favorites, but she always wears bright colors."

I point at the huge yellow flowers. "These?"

"Perfect," she says.

"Are you getting married?" the man asks with the kind of smile that might mean he likes joking with kids.

"In a way," I say.

Together, Naomi Marie and I run back to Dad, Valerie, Brianna, and Loofie, and hand the flowers to Valerie.

"We got these for you for the pictures," Naomi Marie says.

"Happy wedding day," I add.

Valerie smiles, and as she pulls us both into a hug, I think I see tears in her eyes.

Loofie works fast, shooting pictures from different angles, and doesn't even take any pictures of only Dad and Valerie. Every single picture has all five of us in it.

After I hug him good-bye, as we're getting ready for our

bakery-to-bakery road trip, I stop Naomi Marie, because there's something I need to say.

Brianna's already climbing into her booster seat, and Dad's starting the engine, so I blurt it out. "I really am sorry I didn't help you on the DuoTek contest."

"I know," she says. "You already said so."

"Okay. Good. I've never had a sister before. And I want—I just want it to be good." I know she already has a sister and doesn't really need another one. I might have been a little scared she was going to say that to me.

"Oh, we're good," Naomi Marie says. "And I think we'll get even better."

Something that has been pulled tight inside me lets go, like a flower opening its petals toward the sun.

"I'm going to ask you a question," she says. "And I want you to tell me the truth."

Uh-oh. I nod.

She's looking right at me, even though the sun is in her eyes. "That thing you told me to try with Orchid Richardson. Where you study someone to figure them out, the way your mom does, to come up with their costumes. Did you do that with me?"

I feel my lips moving up into a smile. "Did you try it?" I ask. "What costume would Orchid Richardson wear?"

Dad sticks his head out the window like he's going to tell us to hurry up and get in, but when he sees us talking, he pulls his head back in and puts the window back up.

"I'm still working on it, but it's definitely an awful shade of pink. And I'm almost positive it's really uncomfortable. Should I ask what costume I'd be wearing?"

"Sure," I say. I look at her, trying to think of her as my sister; but it's still pretty new to think of her as my friend, so that will have to do for now. "It would be some kind of beautiful sundress you made yourself. You probably dyed it blue and yellow at a museum workshop. It would be exactly, perfectly you."

She smiles at me. Before she can climb into the car, I ask, "So are you happy or scared about all this? Our, you know, new family."

She smiles and says, "It's not *or*, right? It's all about *and*."

Happy *and* scared. She's right.

"We've got this," she says as she climbs into the car. I wonder if she believes that or is just wishing it.

But of course it must be both.

Believing it. And wishing it.

Happy and scared.

But really, right now, what's most important: Shelly Ann's AND Morningstar!

Acknowledgments

Erin Murphy remembered an early attempt at this book and mentioned it at the exact right time to the exact right person. That we all three met on the same day is some kind of wonderful SCBWI miracle.

Kristin Rens has to be the most clear-eyed and encouraging editor in all the land. She never panicked, even when drafts lacked . . . focus, among other things. We thank you wholeheartedly for knowing just what needed doing and trusting that we were up to the task.

Our deepest appreciation to everyone at Balzer + Bray for supporting our Naomis from the very start.

And to our families and friends and our families' friends and our friends' families, thank you for lifting us up when we got low, for calming us down when things went awry, and for making sure we kept ourselves pointed in the right direction. For cheering us on, for believing in the power of stories, and for celebrating with us every step of the way, we are humbled and grateful.

And to our readers: thank you for spending your time with us and our stories. Be the fullness of who you are, and take every opportunity for Shelly Ann's AND Morningstar. (And maybe Yumi's too.)

Olugbemisola Rhuday-Perkovich is the author of the middle grade novel *8th Grade Superzero* and has contributed to the website Brightly and the books *Open Mic: Riffs on Life Between Cultures in Ten Voices* and *Break These Rules: 35 YA Authors on Speaking Up, Standing Out, and Being Yourself*. Like Naomi Marie, she enjoys showing her leadership skills to her younger sister and wishes you could eat cake in the library. She lives with her family in New York City, where she writes, makes things, and needs to get more sleep. Olugbemisola loves to visit with readers and writers like you.

Audrey Vernick is the author of more than a dozen books for young readers, including the picture books *Is Your Buffalo Ready for Kindergarten?* and *First Grade Dropout* and the middle grade novel *Water Balloon*. Like Naomi E., she adores a good bakery and is not fond of her middle name. Audrey enjoys visiting schools to speak with young readers and writers. She lives with her family near the ocean in New Jersey.